EVENING PROPOSAL

PYUN HYE YOUNG

EVENING PROPOSAL

STORIES

Translated by Youngsuk Park and Gloria Cosgrove Smith

DALKEY ARCHIVE PRESS

Originally published in Korean by Moonji Publishing Company in 2011.

Library of Congress Cataloging-in-Publication Data
Identifiers: ISBN 9781628971545
LC record available at https://catalog.loc.gov/

Partially funded by a grant by the Illinois Arts Council, a state agency
Published in collaboration with the Literature Translation Institute of Korea

Dalkey Archive Press publications are, in part, made possible through the support of the University of Houston-Victoria and its programs in creative writing, publishing, and translation.

Dalkey Archive Press
Victoria, TX / McLean, IL / Dublin
www.dalkeyarchive.com

Cover design and composition by Mikhail Iliatov
Printed on permanent/durable acid-free paper

Contents

Commentary

RABBIT'S TOMB

A RABBIT. IT was a rabbit. At the faint rustling sound, the man turned and glanced toward the bushes thinking at first that it was a ball of white yarn. Or perhaps a white dog staring at him, but it was the eyes that convinced him. It was a rabbit. He crouched on his knees in front of it. The red eyes were mesmerizing. He stared at them, forgetting for a second that they were the eyes of a special breed of rabbit. All that occurred to him at this moment was that there existed a life besides his own in this world, a life so worn out and weary, its eyes had actually turned red. This thought gave him a surge of comfort. But that such a life had been abandoned in a dark park for so long that its white fur had started to look like dirty trash made him feel bitter.

Certainly, the rabbit had been abandoned. There was no way it'd been born and bred in the park. Rabbits like this had once been sensationally popular pets for city children. Now, however, parents were secretly abandoning them. As with so many fads, no one knew for sure what had caused the rabbit craze. But commercials starring a well-known, healthy-looking, middle-aged doctor might well have been influential enough to get it going. This doctor claimed that he was raising a breed of rabbit that didn't grow very large, and that he himself had become a vegetarian as a result of observing its eating habits. Parents may also have been influenced by an amusing animated cartoon on television that featured a charming, witty rabbit with heavy-lidded eyes that suggested it was in possession of a unique personality. A clever picture book about a suicidal rabbit had also been published. It portrayed a rabbit that was neither worn out nor weary, but merely so bored and tired of living that it was playfully attempting suicide.

Children had become tired of dogs and cats, of baby chicks that died so easily, of monstrously prolific hamsters. Street vendors in front of schools still sold the same old machine-hatched baby chicks, but now they were also selling these mini rabbits in paper boxes—baby rabbits that were not yet weaned. Parents were wary, but they were told that raising a rabbit wasn't at all complicated and that pet rabbits typically thrived on rabbit food alone. Furthermore, a famous professor claimed that a person could learn a great deal from watching rabbits. Thus parents' apprehensions were allayed. When one or two households began adopting rabbits, other children dared to beg their parents for them too, and parents could find no reason to refuse. According to a survey conducted this year by a company that sold dry alfalfa hay for rabbit food, there was an eightfold increase in the number of households with pet rabbits compared to the year before.

As is true with any pet, however, actually raising the rabbits didn't turn out to be quite as easy, interesting, or convenient as anticipated. Besides, none of these rabbits were such model vegetarians. Like other pets raised in houses in this city, these rabbits ate only a fixed amount of hard food or dry grass. This was convenient enough, but there were none of those small delights to be reaped from watching them nibble on carrots or other vegetable matter. It was difficult to imagine how on earth anyone could learn to be a vegetarian from observing a rabbit that ate only hard food and dry grass. It was perplexing. It had been asserted that when they grew up, they could be fed fruits and vegetables. However, it soon became apparent that feeding them these foods if they were even just a little wet could be lethal, so their feedings had to be kept under close control.

Thus the rabbits turned out to be parasitic dependents, picky eaters that consumed expensive food and required other costly items for their maintenance. Unlike cats or dogs, they were neither friendly nor affectionate. They could hardly be considered pets, let alone companions. They could justifiably be treated as cows or pigs when one considered their feeding costs, but unlike cows or pigs they didn't even provide good meat. Owners reported that they had to be fed extremely carefully. The slightest imbalance in their food could cause foul-smelling excrement. Also, they shed their fur, which made you cough. And if you so much as dared to glance at their newborn babies, they retaliated with, as the familiar saying goes, looks that could kill. These rabbits didn't even commit suicide as the one in the picture book did.

The children soon became bored, and the parents were unwilling to take responsibility for these rabbits, which could become family members for as long six or eight years. According to the Guinness Book of World Records, the longest surviving rabbit lived for eighteen years. Hence, during a rabbit's life span of six, eight, or possibly eighteen years, a child who'd once begged his parents for a rabbit could conceivably finish high school, enter college, get married, and start a life of his own. Besides which, the economy was so perpetually unpredictable that no one could know when there might be another downturn that would make them feel like getting rid of one of their family members. It was simply infeasible to maintain a rabbit for six or more years when all it could do was chew hard food or dry grass with its long teeth.

Still, one couldn't say raising a rabbit was a total waste of time. If there was one thing to be learned from raising a rabbit, it was that being stared at for a considerable length of time completely without expression could eventually incite anyone to hatred. This phenomenon often resulted in one of the parents, usually the father, pretending to take the rabbit for a walk in the park, where, in the dark of night, he would release the rabbit into the bushes. Soon after it disappeared, or even before it disappeared, the father would promptly head for home. Without slowing his pace, he might look over his shoulder once or twice, trying to ignore the voice of his conscience by convincing himself that the rabbit wasn't really being abandoned, it was merely lost. He might even tell himself that being abandoned wasn't necessarily so terrible. The park after all was like a spot of wilderness in the city. The rabbit would know which grass to eat. It could find a soft place to sleep and in time, it would get sick and die just like any ordinary gnat, pigeon, crow, mouse, ant, or other living creature. Walking home, the father might momentarily have the feeling that something was missing. When he arrived, he would look into the cage to be sure that the rabbit hadn't somehow returned. Seeing the cage empty, he'd be relieved. With one of his hands, he would brush the rabbit fur from his chest.

And here was one of those abandoned rabbits. The man knelt and caressed its soft white fur. He felt its back beating gently to the rhythm of its pulse. The rabbit remained calm, as if it were used to being handled like this. The man was charmed by the pulsing of its veins and the slow rhythm of its breathing. Returning home with the rabbit, he hurried to order a cage. Only then did he realize that he should never have picked up an abandoned rabbit in the park because he too would eventually have to abandon it. He was scheduled to stay no more than six months in this city, and some of that time had already passed. When he finished this temporary assignment, he would return home. Then, just as others in this city had done before him, he too would have to secretly abandon this rabbit in the dark of night.

*

The man's work was simple enough. He had to organize documents from his home city, scan information related to it, list it on a simple form, and submit it to the person in charge. While filling in the forms he felt like a student detained at a teacher's office to write an essay outlining his wrongdoings.

Similarly, the person in charge always smiled and thanked him, receiving the document as if it were an essay outlining his wrongdoings. Seeing the same smile and hearing the same words day after day from the person in charge, regardless of the content of the document, the man assumed that this way of smiling and speaking must be part of the person in charge's job description. He seemed to appreciate very little about the content or quality of the man's work, since he always immediately turned around and tossed the document on top of a huge pile of other documents. Still, the man worried about possible errors in the documents he submitted. He was concerned that errors might cause serious economic, diplomatic, or cultural problems in relations between the two cities. He slept badly at night, even having nightmares in which the representatives of the two cities were at odds with each other due to inaccurate statistics that voided their contractual agreement. In reality, no such thing ever happened. Days passed smoothly. He continued to gather information from faxes and the Internet. He continued to fill out forms and submit them to the person in charge.

Once he intentionally recorded incorrect totals in his report, and as usual the person in charge simply tossed the document on top of the huge pile. Fretfully, the man returned to his seat ready with a corrected copy in a submission cover. He waited until closing time, but the person in charge said nothing. Time passed, and there were no major problems regarding negotiations or agreements between the two cities. The man finally relaxed. He stopped having bad dreams. From then on, he interpreted the sound of his documents being tossed on top of the pile merely as a signal that his day's work was completed. He returned to his seat to kill time fidgeting with papers and organizing his desk. He decided that if anyone should ever inquire as to what kind of work he did, he would reply that he worked to establish cooperation and integration between two cities that had been enemies in long standing. But as it turned out, never once during his whole dispatched time did a single soul ever bother to ask.

He remembered the words of the older alumnus who had told him on the phone that he would be collecting information that would be useful for various purposes.

"In general, you will be functioning to build a bridge between two cities."

"But what kind of information should be collected?" he'd asked, and immediately realized that this type of question wouldn't be appreciated. He could almost see the older alumnus looking at him as if he were a three-year-old child crying to be fed. He regretted his impulsiveness. He should have inquired in a different manner.

"I have collected some information. This information may be useful in some ways but totally useless in others. This is what I understand about the work. Is this acceptable?"

That was how, he realized, he should have addressed his mentor. That was how the older alumnus had taught him to behave in the early stages of his company life. "Any information will work," the older alumnus unexpectedly and gently responded. "Selecting and making decisions about the usefulness of the information is the role for the person in charge to play. All you have to do is collect. In other words, you should think of yourself as a sort of hunting dog."

A hunting dog? This presented yet another problem. How does one think of oneself as a hunting dog? But he didn't ask this question. He kept quiet and listened.

"You must catch and bring back the targeted object," the older alumnus continued. "It's as simple as that. What to catch and what to do with it afterwards, broil, boil, throw away or stuff, making these decisions isn't the role for a hunting dog nosing through the woods. It is for the owner, who orders and watches. Therefore, all the dog has to do is run in the field with all his might—even to his death—until he makes the catch."

"Well, that's not a very amusing figure of speech."

"Ha, ha, isn't it true, though? Sorry. Really it's not you but I who feels this way," the older alumnus shyly apologized. Judging by this metaphor, the older alumnus felt no no differently than he did. Now he understood. Neither of them was the owner of the hunting dog.

If the appointment had been for a longer period of time, he would have hesitated, but since it was only six months, he agreed to take the dispatched work. The older alumnus, in a strangely reluctant voice, thanked him for making that decision. Later, however, he would come to realize that he'd actually been appointed before he'd made his decision—a realization that clearly indicated to him his place in the hierarchy. This appointment convinced him that he was of little worth.

Since the information he could obtain about the city was limited and he rarely had contact with anyone, he spent most of his time at his desk, shuffling papers and examining their contents. As he had plenty of time and little work to do, he worked as slowly as possible. He walked hurriedly when crossing the office or the hallways in order to appear busy and not raise suspicions that he had too little to do. His wasn't the type of work where mistakes occurred, except for deliberate ones. He didn't make mistakes, so that he wouldn't have to spend time correcting errors. If the person in charge had asked him to correct errors on a submitted paper or to somehow supplement it, he would have gladly agreed to have something more to do. But this never happened. His work received no comment. No part of it was ever cited as being especially well done or as requiring supplementation, nor was it ever mentioned that there were too many typos or errors to count.

He had no complaints about the person in charge. On the contrary, he was rather fond of him, if just because he was the only person he conversed with in the office, and the formal greeting when he submitted his documents was the only recognition he received. In fact, he hardly spoke all day long. He said hello to the superintendent of his building when on occasion he ran into him. But otherwise, his only words were, "here is what I've done today," which he said whenever he submitted his documents.

It seemed to him that all his coworkers were so busy that they never moved except during their lunch hours. They sat in front of well-organized desks, staring at their computer monitors as though watching interesting movies, or they stared at papers on their desks with their heads inclined as though they were asleep. Even during the lunch hour, instead of noisily flooding out in companionable groups, each individual bought a lunch box of his own preference from the row of food trucks in front of the building, found a seat by himself, and quietly ate alone.

At times he left his desk to submit a paper to the person in charge and, pretending that he had other work to do as well, he deliberately walked across the whole length of the office space, which was as huge as a plaza. The office was like an enormous beehive composed of endless divisions subdivided by cubicles. It was arranged by region and city, and each cubicle was marked with a section indicator and a seat number so that it could be easily located. Large directories, like those at performing arts theaters, were posted next to the entrance door.

The day after he found the rabbit, he was about to submit a document but, at the last moment, quickly put it behind his back instead. The person in charge had been just about to take it from him, and wasn't pleased with this gesture. He stopped smiling and glared at his subordinate, who quickly realized that such playfulness wasn't deemed appropriate. Confused and unsure of himself, he nevertheless gathered his courage, opened his mouth, and asked his question.

"Is there by any chance anyone among the workers here who is raising a rabbit?"

"A rabbit?"

"Yes, do you happen to know?" he asked as he pulled the document from behind his back and handed it over. "I'm looking for some help. I happen to have a rabbit, and having been dispatched here not too long ago, I'm having a difficult time making friends."

The person in charge took the document from him and tossed it on top of the pile.

"Anyone can raise a rabbit. It's easy. There should be no need for special help. Furthermore, most of the people here are on temporary dispatched terms. Dispatched work isn't that unusual." Having said this, the person in charge was about to turn away from him to avoid dealing with the matter any longer, but the man was determined to get an answer.

"Who? Who is someone like that?" he asked hurriedly.

"What do you mean 'like that'?"

"I want to know who has raised a rabbit. And who is a dispatched worker?" he said, pleased that he was at least being listened to.

"I wouldn't know. No one would know. As I already told you, a rabbit is an animal anyone can raise, and all of us are similarly dispatched—just for different time periods."

Having spoken these words, the person in charge lowered his head to make it quite clear he didn't wish to deal with the man any further. Losing hope, the man stared down at his superior's head of dark hair, which was meticulously parted on the right side. Then he returned to his cubicle. Based on what he'd just heard, he suspected that many of his co-workers must be raising rabbits. Possibly among them was the very person who'd abandoned the rabbit he'd found. If they were all dispatched workers, one of them, or perhaps one from a previous period, could have abandoned it. Exactly as he would mercilessly abandon it when his own dispatched term expired.

*

He knocked at the door. "Are you in, Sir?" No one answered. He banged on the door again and called out, "Are you there?" and again no one answered. He sank down in front of the door, but the wall was hard and the floor was cold, so he immediately stood up again. He knew very well that it made no sense to expect someone to be inside, or to expect that the older alumnus would ever show up, no matter how long he sat and waited. Nonetheless, he went to his place each day, knocked at the door, convinced himself there'd be no answer, and then returned again. Some days he kicked against the door and pounded on it with his fists and shouted in vain: "I know you're in there! Open the door!" Other days he would stand there sniffing for an odor. There never was an odor. But he wasn't sure whether or not this was a good sign. Perhaps the fact that he believed this wasn't a good sign was in fact a sign that he wasn't thinking clearly.

He remembered that it was shortly after his own arrival in the city that the older alumnus was supposed to have disappeared from the office. He'd visited the personnel office and asked where he might be able to track him down. The person in charge there tried to remember. He browsed the long roster of names, and finally said that the older alumnus was absent without leave.

"Absent without leave?" the man asked.

The person in charge simply nodded as though this wasn't at all serious. The man remembered working with the older alumnus. Although it hadn't been for a very long time, he would never have thought of him as the sort to be absent without leave. He was the kind of worker who was conscientious and efficient during office hours and diligent in his attendance. He'd been a role model in every aspect of office life. The older alumnus had taught him how to fulfill his job description. It was also the older alumnus who'd taught him how to handle firsthand information so that it would benefit himself alone, by keeping the good news to himself, while circulating disparaging news quickly to the rest of the world. When he was newly employed and handing in documents that he'd been ordered to fill out, the older alumnus always perused them immediately.

"Hmm. Good. However, this part should be touched up," the older alumnus would say and return them to him unaware—or perhaps only pretending to be unaware—that he'd been given the nickname "However" by the other younger workers. Having retrieved the document, the man himself wasn't always able to plunge right into correcting it. Newly employed as he was, he had to tend to trivial matters urgently required by others from far and near, leaving him no time for correcting a document that had already been submitted. All he could manage to do was rearrange the information listed and increase the margins between the sections before handing it in again. He would then be complimented.

"I regret that this didn't come a little earlier. However, it looks much better with your corrections," he'd be told.

He'd felt embarrassed that he didn't have the older man's address and so couldn't contact him, especially since he was the one who'd advised him to take this temporary assignment. He tried phoning the personnel office several times. He left memos, but received no news in return. Finally, after several failed attempts, he'd met with the person in charge of the personnel office, who insisted that private information couldn't be released. He pleaded until he obtained the address. He discovered that it wasn't far from his own residence, and every day after work he stopped by, knocked on the door and called out the older man's name. Time after time, he was convinced that there was no sign of human existence. Time after time, he returned home deeply resenting the older alumnus for disappearing so soon after he'd embarked on this new assignment.

In the beginning, he'd feed the rabbit when he got home. But besides feeding it with hard food, he had absolutely nothing to do with it. He didn't take it out of its cage to let it run free around the house, or brush its fur, or clean its cage, or hold it to his chest and caress it. He became tired of it. One day he'd pour out a large batch of the hard food for it to gorge on to its heart's content. Other times, he'd forget to feed it and let it go hungry for days. The fact was he'd picked up the rabbit to care for it only during this period of temporary work. If he'd been required to stay longer or permanently in this city, he'd never have brought it home with him. At most he'd be responsible for it for only a few months. Because he wasn't the rabbit's permanent caretaker, he felt no need to concern himself with its emotional or physical health. After all, sooner or later, the rabbit would have to be abandoned.

He hardly ever went anywhere in the evenings. His daily routine in this city was to go to work, and on his way home to knock at the older alumnus's door. Sensing no movement inside, and not smelling any strange odor, he'd then go to a convenience store to purchase a simple meal for his supper. And that was all. He had been going out walking occasionally after supper to the neighborhood park where he'd found the rabbit. But then one evening after watching the news, he ceased to do so.

An accident was reported. It had occurred in the city shortly after he arrived. A man wearing a training uniform bearing the name Morning Soccer Club in large letters had, by accident, whirled a sword at a group of citizens who were enjoying a leisurely Sunday afternoon in the park. Three people were killed and nine were injured. The Morning Soccer Clubs of various regions were falsely accused. For a while they stopped their morning soccer games and took the name off their uniforms. After changing their names, they resumed playing morning, day, and evening. It was yet to be determined how such an accident could have happened so that preventive measures could be taken.

Then a video predicting another killing spree was sent to the broadcasting company and was run on the evening news. It went viral on the Internet, and the man watched it almost all day long. No one else mentioned it, but he felt sure that many of his coworkers were also watching it. The video depicted a masked man, his upper body naked, yelling and swinging a sword whose edge was seen only as a blur on the screen. Specialists analyzed the voice and determined that the man was in his thirties or forties. That was the only available information. So it was anyone's guess who this person might be.

The image was quite clear, suggesting that the video had been filmed with a fixed camera. Every so often the masked man with his whirling sword and naked upper body stood up to smoke a cigarette or go to the bathroom. At these times, only the empty room was visible. As he watched the video, the man felt that the room seemed somehow familiar. Then he realized that the shape, the color, the arrangement of the furniture, the characterless white wallpaper, in short the whole interior, was identical to that of his own room. His heart raced. The building he lived in had twenty-eight floors. Each floor had twenty-five apartments. He didn't know who his neighbors were. The older alumnus had recommended this place to him, and he assumed that others from his office also lived there.

The video was broadcast on the national news for several days, but nothing happened. A specialist appeared on television and said he deplored the incident. He concluded from his analysis that a man with a strong tendency toward exhibitionism had made the video. That was nothing special. Anyone could have done that much deploring and analyzing. Since the man in the video was only a potential criminal, the police made little effort to search for him. They merely warned people to be cautious because another such accident could unpredictably occur anywhere.

The man began to fear his neighbors. It occurred to him that he had no way of knowing if one of them had taken off his shirt, grabbed a kitchen knife, and made the video. To avoid running into anyone, he didn't open his door when he heard the sound of a neighbor's door opening or closing. He frequently checked the hallway through his fisheye lens. Occasionally, he heard the elevator stop on his floor but then saw no one in the hall. This frightened him. He had no way of knowing if a man in his thirties or forties was hiding out there with a kitchen knife just waiting for somebody to appear. If he saw anyone approaching him when he arrived at the gate of his apartment complex, he quickly turned and walked in the opposite direction. He cringed when his sudden turning startled the person behind him even more than he had been startled. He avoided being alone in the elevator with a stranger by quickly punching the button to close the door if he saw someone coming toward him. Then one day when he was approaching the elevator, he saw someone else hurriedly pushing the button. Seeing this made him less fearful of his neighbors. It also made him realize that he himself was a stranger, and that his fear was no different from anyone else's. It was, he decided, completely due to his being unfamiliar with this city. The mystery would eventually be solved, but by then this temporary work assignment of his would be over and done with.

For the first time, he wanted to talk in earnest with someone about the man in the video and about the fact that the man's room was exactly like his. It had been a long time since he'd felt such a need. He hadn't realized the extent to which he'd gotten used to being alone. Since moving to this city the longest conversation he'd had, other than those with the person in charge, consisted of his asking a shop owner the price of polished rice because it didn't have a price tag. He wasn't entirely aware that he hadn't talked with anyone for such a long time. He'd been so frightened by the man in the video, and so busy envisioning himself as a possible victim, his undiscovered body left rotting in some narrow room, that he had made no effort to meet anyone in this city. Now he wanted to talk with someone about his feelings, but the only person he could think of was the older alumnus who'd disappeared. The situation was hopeless. He grew impatient, and one day he asked the person in charge whether he'd seen the video. The only response he received was that the whole matter wasn't of much concern and that such accidents frequently happened in the city.

"But the room in the video looks exactly the same as mine," he whispered.

"If it makes you feel any better," the person in charge said slowly raising his head from his work, "it also looks the same as mine." That meant that all the single-residence apartments in this city were roughly the same. He felt somewhat consoled by this, but it really didn't make him feel a great deal better.

Eventually the shock caused by the video faded, the city quieted down, and he felt that his neurotic dread had been rather shameful. Fewer people went out into the streets than before, but otherwise nothing happened. Sometimes at night an ambulance howled by carrying a patient in need of emergency care, but these emergencies weren't caused by the kind of accident that had been feared. These nightly screaming sirens signified only regular police patrol, not disasters.

*

It wasn't until almost closing time at the office that he became aware that the person in charge had been replaced. He finished his usual easy job of organizing and totaling up the meager sum of information he'd gathered on his city that day, but when he went to submit it, he discovered a different person sitting at the desk.

"Where has the person in charge gone?" he asked.

"From now on I'm the one in charge," the new occupant of the seat replied. The words were spoken in a clipped and frugal tone and accompanied by a smile. The voice may have been different from that of his predecessor, but the pitch was similar. He realized then that the person formerly in charge was just another dispatched worker, and that this change of personnel would make no difference at all. In the days that followed, the man continued to submit his orderly documents exactly as before, every afternoon. And every afternoon, this new person took the documents with a smile, placed them on top of the pile at the corner of his desk without looking at them, and went on with his work. The man interpreted this repetition as a sign that he could leave the office soon afterward. He returned to his seat to get ready to go home. Up to that point, everything went on more or less the same as before.

There was one thing that did change, though. He began to look around the office more often than he had previously. He observed that all the workers were dressed in basic black suits and white shirts. Some were wearing their jackets and some were not, so that from a distance the office space resembled a *Go* game board with a mix of black and white stones placed on it. He stood up from his seat and lifting his head, he counted the number of white shirts and black jackets. Then, as if he were playing *omok*[1], he tried to find five of the same color in a row in any direction. When he had done so, a mischievous smile crossed his face, and he sat back down in his seat feeling like a winner. He played this game exactly five times each day, soon after arriving in the office in the morning, right before lunchtime, right after

1 Five stones in a row

returning from lunch, at three or four o'clock in the afternoon, and once again before leaving the office. Most of the time he found five cubes filled in, and sometimes even as many as twelve.

He noted again that his coworkers rarely left their seats, moving only to go to the bathrooms or to the persons in charge of their regions. He wondered why on earth they remained so firmly fixed in place. According to the older alumnus, they were doing the same tasks he did, gathering information on each of their regions. But the older alumnus didn't know how they were working or what information they were gathering.

"They are specialists, like you. They're better informed than anyone else concerning the city they're responsible for. But that is all they know, and that is the only problem."

He sensed that the older alumnus didn't know much about their job descriptions either, and he refrained from asking further questions. Since then, he'd thought of new questions, but because the older alumnus was absent without leave, they remained unanswered.

Now someone was knocking at his partition. He looked up to see the person in charge. In all the time he'd worked there, the person in charge had never before come to see him. This, then, was somewhat curious, but he was thankful for the visit, and thought how fortunate it was that he was hard at work concentrating on a document at that particular moment. He smiled shyly. He was handed a roster and, in a caring tone of voice, told to look for a junior member to assist him with his duties. He was already quite aware that his six-month assignment was drawing to a close, and he wondered if there was some process in place whereby another person would take over his workload.

On the phone, with uncertainty in his voice, the junior colleague, whom he was to train, asked what sort of information he'd be expected to collect. He told him that it didn't really matter. The junior colleague replied that he'd like to take some time to make his decision. He made not the slightest effort to tell the junior colleague that his decision was of no consequence, that the matter had already been decided and announced. He simply said in a less than enthusiastic voice, intended to reveal his displeasure, that the junior colleague could do whatever he wished. The next day the junior colleague phoned to explain that this temporary assignment would be like a long voyage for him and that he was willing to take the dispatched work. He gladly thanked the junior colleague for making his decision, answered questions regarding housing and the job description, and provided other necessary advice as well. At that point, he suddenly realized he was using the same words that the older alumnus had spoken to him when he received the announcement of his assignment. This in turn reminded him of the hunting dog metaphor, which he also relayed to the junior colleague. After he hung up, he felt embarrassed and burst out laughing.

He didn't show up for work on the first day that the junior colleague came to the office. He knew that his replacement could easily find his cubicle by consulting the seating chart posted at the entrance, and that he could start his work quite easily without any help. Had he been forced to explain his absence, he'd have blamed the rabbit. The rabbit had filled its stomach with all the dry food he'd tossed into its dish the day before and then escaped its cage during the night and defecated everywhere. He woke to an odor of excrement that made him vomit. He cleared his nose of rabbit fur and stood by the open window until the horrible odor, which seemed to have saturated his whole body, gradually faded away. Then, realizing that he was already late for work, he decided that, rather than be tardy, he'd simply be absent for the first time—just for this one day.

The next day, although the odor had diminished, he once more decided not to go to work. He realized that his absence the day before had caused no disturbance at the office, and consequently saw no reason why he couldn't stay away for a second day. If someone were to ask him the reason for his absence, he felt he'd rather not explain about the rabbit. That would be too embarrassing. He decided instead that he would say he'd grown tired of the whole process of examining material, filling out forms, submitting reports, and seeing his submissions summarily discarded. He thought such work could easily be neglected a time or two without causing any great trouble. He settled on this response, though it soon became clear that no one was ever going to question him.

As a consequence, he stopped going to the office altogether. But now that he was staying at home all day he didn't know what to do with himself. The only thing he could possibly do at home was watch the rabbit—the rabbit whose red eyes were still so disturbing. He ended up covering its cage with a black cloth. Then he sat down at his desk and started to do the same work he'd have been doing in the office. He searched the Internet for information about his city, organized the information, and filled out the forms. His work at home was no different, but it pleased him that he didn't have to put on a white shirt. He wore the same clothes he slept in, baggy pajama bottoms and stretched out tee shirts. He smoked freely while on the Internet, and got up from his desk five times during the day just as he had in the office. The first time he sprang up, he laughed loudly and went to the bathroom without needing to. The second time he smiled bashfully and went to get a drink of water. The third time he beat his head. The fourth time he felt like crying and the fifth time he did cry. At the regular office closing time, he switched off his computer and stopped his work in progress. That was the correct thing to do, because he knew dispatched workers were not paid overtime.

One day, when he was considering removing the black cloth from the rabbit cage, he heard a soft knocking at his door. He didn't answer.

"Are you in, Sir?" a voice called. With the voice coming through the door as it was, he could not recognize it. He tip-toed quietly to the door and peered through the fisheye lens. The person who had been knocking had already turned to leave. He saw only the back of a black jacket, and caught a glimpse of a white shirt collar, neither of which provided a real clue as to the person's identity. There were too many people in the city—not only his colleagues but also other office workers, sales people, missionaries—who dressed in this same fashion.

He carried on working at home just as he had at the office. He worried somewhat as payday approached, but when he checked his bank balance he saw that his salary had been deposited to his account in a timely manner. From then on, he took it for granted that he'd receive his salary whether he worked at home or in the office, just as long as he made the same progress. He withdrew a portion of his salary and went to the convenience store, where he purchased food for himself and the rabbit.

Each day, about ten minutes after the office had closed, there was a knock at his door. He remained quiet. He didn't respond. One day the knock was soft, like someone gently tapping at a bathroom door. Another day it was a rough, angry pounding, and still another day it sounded as though someone was sitting out in front of the door murmuring or pleading. Perhaps it was because the voice was coming through the tight entrance door and couldn't be heard accurately that it sounded more like complaining than someone eagerly wishing to see him.

The end of the period scheduled for his dispatched work was approaching. Little by little, he began packing his belongings. He had accumulated a great deal in a few months, but he discarded everything he'd acquired while residing in this city, and packed the rest in his trunk. He'd leave with the same things he had arrived with. At exactly midnight when his dispatched period ended, he calculated the management fee for his apartment building and gave it to the building superintendent. Then, carrying the rabbit, he dragged his trunk outside. Because the rabbit had been fed irregularly, its weight had fluctuated, but now, as he held it to his chest, it felt the same to him as when he first picked it up.

He placed it in the bushes in the park. The rabbit made no attempt to jump back to him, try to cling to his trousers or follow him. It simply disappeared into the bushes, as though it already knew what it was supposed to do. He made up his mind not to turn around even if it gave out a pitiful cry, but he never heard a sound. He brushed the rabbit fur from his hands and dragged his rattling trunk out of the park. All over the world, he told himself, animals are abandoned.

EVENING PROPOSAL

KIM'S FRIEND ORDERED the funeral wreath. It had been more than ten years since Kim had seen this friend, who now recognized his voice on the phone. Perhaps he was an inconsiderate person, or merely acting like one, as he completely neglected the formality of greeting Kim or inquiring about his well-being. Without introduction, he simply described the condition of an ill, bedridden man. Only after listening for a few moments did Kim realize that the person on the phone was a friend from long ago, and that the ill, bedridden person was an elderly man whom Kim had often visited during the period when he was corresponding with this friend.

Kim paid little attention to the man's incessant chattering on the phone. Instead, he wondered how he'd obtained his new phone number, since he had taken over the florist shop only quite recently. He was also struggling to determine just how old the elderly dying man would be now. He'd have been surprised to hear that he'd already died, but hearing that he was still alive was also quite surprising. He didn't mention this to his friend, not wishing to seem unsympathetic, especially now, when they were talking to each other again after such a long time. Kim couldn't remember exactly, but he felt the elderly man must have reached an age at which no one would be surprised at his passing.

"He is unconscious, breathing with the aid of a respirator as unconscious people do, and exhaling slowly," the friend reported. "Every time he exhales, I nod my head cheering him on, but then I look at the clock."

Kim was unable to tell whether the friend's voice expressed grief or disappointment.

"The doctor said it was unlikely that he'd still be alive this afternoon."

The friend paused for a moment. It seemed as though he was waiting for Kim to say something, possibly to ask the location of the hospital so he could visit, to express sympathy, or perhaps to provide some words of comfort. But Kim said nothing. The friend sighed.

"Please do me a favor with the wreath," he said.

Kim agreed somewhat reluctantly, as though he had no choice. He was thinking that doing this friend a favor quite likely meant he wouldn't be paid, and it wasn't as if they were really friends. Their relationship was so tenuous that they could easily be considered strangers. But it seemed mercenary to be dickering about money when the elderly man was dying.

Without mentioning anything about payment, the friend then asked for Kim's mobile number and gave him the name of the funeral home, which was located in a town Kim wasn't familiar with. Merely to continue the conversation, Kim was about to ask why the mortuary was located in that town, but he changed his mind. In a telephone conversation such as this, taking place out of nowhere after more than ten years, there was really only one thing Kim wanted to know. How had this old acquaintance obtained his phone number? Their only connection was that they had worked for the same company for a short time. It would even be difficult for them to recognize each other in a photo taken at a company event. In such a photo, they would anyway have been standing quite far apart, and their relationship had definitely not changed over these past ten years.

"You are coming to the funeral, aren't you?" the friend asked. Kim hesitated and, before he could answer, the friend added, "Of course you are. Anyway, who else should we call?"

His tone of voice indicated that the matter wasn't open for discussion. Kim was about to explain that he wasn't in touch with any of their acquaintances from ten years ago, when this friend, not waiting for a response, and as though he was thoroughly displeased with Kim's reluctance, suddenly raised his voice.

"Never mind! I'll do it!" he said. Then he gave Kim the name of the organization that was sending the wreath. It was an organization Kim had never heard of. Feeling that it would be rude not to inquire, Kim forced himself to ask what this organization did. But the friend abruptly hung up on him, saying that he had to return to the hospital. There were no goodbyes at the end of their conversation, just as there had been no greetings at the beginning.

Kim wondered if he was somehow responsible for his friend's cold, rude behavior or if it was merely the man's personality. He reflected on past events and was reminded of some letters his friend had written. This was during the period when Kim decided to resign from their company, which was under legal management as a result of severe financial pressure caused by the company's inadequate expansion. The employees had voluntarily accepted a wage reduction to stabilize the company's financial situation when Kim was recommended for a position in another company in another city. The person who recommended him was the same elderly man who was now dying, and this friend had criticized him for taking the new position. He claimed that

Kim had no sense of camaraderie and accused him of being self-ish and calculating.

Kim was told about this criticism by another person with whom he'd had no contact for a long time. Criticizing a person for being selfish makes no sense, Kim thought. Everyone is self-ish. If his friend had been recommended for the position, he wouldn't have hesitated to take it. But his friend was hurt by what he felt was Kim's uncaring attitude. He sent letters to Kim's new company citing several mistakes Kim had made. The result was that Kim was talked about behind his back for a time, until the whole matter gradually blew over. As a result of this experi-ence, Kim concluded that friendship had nothing to do with affection, but was a feeling valid only when it reaped benefits for one of the persons involved. He calmly recalled the event and the scars it had inflicted, but the process of remembering did leave him sad and resentful about his long-forgotten past.

He wrote the name of the funeral home on the upper part of a memo where orders for items and their places of delivery were haphazardly scribbled. He'd have remembered these without looking at them, but seeing them now reminded him that he also had other orders to attend to. Not that they had to be attended to before doing anything else, but certainly they did have to be taken care of. Not to mention other urgent events might arise at any time, if not today, then tomorrow, or even in the next five minutes. It was impossible to predict. That is what self-employment is like.

He tried to find someone who could deliver the wreath and the gift money that he'd donate for the funeral expenses. Considering the elderly man's age, even though Kim didn't know exactly what it was, he imagined his funeral could take place at any moment. So it was appropriate to be prepared for mourning.

According to the friend, the elderly man had been unconscious and unable to recognize anyone for a long while. Even if Kim hurried to get to the hospital, he might not be able to arrive before the man died. Realizing this filled him with compassion for dying humanity in general, but his feelings were not at all personal. After transferring to the other company, Kim had felt an obligation to the elderly man and expressed his gratitude with greetings and worthwhile gifts. One year, it was a box of apples for the Harvest Moon Holiday, and for the Lunar New Year Holiday a basket of dry shitake mushrooms. Another year, he gave a box of pears of superior quality for the Lunar New Year and a box of *Hallabong*[2] oranges for the Harvest Moon Holiday. And now, now there would be the wreath for which he'd surely not reap any remuneration. His gratitude had been great, but not great enough to remember after all this time.

*

The funeral home was in a town three hundred and eighty kilometers to the south. Kim was annoyed.

"The news of someone's death shouldn't be sent out to those who have been out of touch for over ten years," he said, frowning. He tried hard to think of someone to call, but everyone he phoned was occupied with other matters. They had important appointments or responsibilities that couldn't be postponed.

"No, the news of a person's death should be sent out far and wide," said the man who ran the florist shop next door to Kim's, "because it too often happens that someone who hasn't heard of a friend's death will come up to you and ask about him as though he's still alive. This happens, you know. I lost my high school buddy of thirty years. Physically, he was the strongest of any of us. Some of our friends still don't know he passed, and

2 A type of oranges raised in Jeju Island

they ask after him. When I tell them he's dead, I realize he's gone all over again." He swallowed his words as he remembered his dead friend. "I wore this to his funeral," he added sorrowfully, handing the black jacket to Kim. Kim nodded.

He didn't really understand the man's sorrow, but after hearing this story about his having had this buddy for thirty years, he was able to guess the florist's age fairly precisely. Until then, he had thought of him as being much older than he actually was on account of his graying hair.

"But this jacket is too big for you, and too old," the man said to Kim.

"It's okay. It really doesn't matter with this kind of jacket," Kim replied, despite the fact that the long sleeves completely covered the back of his hands.

"You're right. It's not as if you're going for an interview," the man said, nodding his head, but he advised Kim to fold the sleeves back twice.

Kim was about fifteen centimeters shorter than the average man. He recalled that he had stopped growing when he turned fourteen. His father had passed away then, and for some time Kim believed that he'd stopped growing because of the emotional shock of his father's death. It wasn't until years later that he realized he was wrong. One day, as a grown man, he went to see a traditional doctor about unbearable pain he had in his shoulder. In the doctor's office, he happened to see a poster on the wall that read: "How to Estimate the Maximum Possible Height of One's Growth." The method involved using the heights of both parents and going through several steps of simple calculations. He used his father's height based on his mother's dim memory of his being one hand span taller than she was. Although it wasn't supposed to be exact, the result of his calculation showed Kim's maximum possible height as only four centimeters taller than his present height. Kim smiled sadly remembering this.

He recalled his childhood, when his father's sudden death forced his mother to work three shifts at a nearby factory, leaving him home alone. His friends teased him about being short, and he often got into trouble because he had too much time to kill. He also blamed his father's death for the disorderly path his life had taken, and mercilessly accused his father of abandoning his family and leaving him with nothing but this meager height. He realized now how wrong he was about all of this.

As he started his car and was about to leave, Kim remembered his dinner date with the woman. He could postpone the date for one or two hours, but even then he probably still wouldn't get back in time. He'd already broken this date with her twice. He apologized to her for his carelessness, and she, as usual, said she understood his situation. Kim sensed that she was concealing her disappointment behind her carefully articulated response, and this displeased him. Instead of being angry, she expressed curiosity about what he had for lunch and how he'd spent his weekend. She often wanted to talk about incidents in her daily life and to discuss matters that required her to make a decision.

Each time she attempted such conversations, however, Kim suddenly had a customer to take care of and would have to hang up right away. A few days later, when she called again, it seemed as though she'd hesitated before picking up the phone to ask how he was. Then she became embarrassed at Kim's unfriendly response. At a loss, she began to spew out words that were far from courteous. When he had a customer and needed to hang up, she hurriedly bid him goodbye in an ambiguous tone of voice that expressed both relief and sorrow for his having to hang up and her not having time to make amends for what she'd said. Later, when he was busy, or even in his free time, he'd be reminded of her face. It was always expressionless, her mouth sealed shut even when she sat among a group of people on a social occasion. She was a quiet woman who every now and then would suddenly make some inane comment which elicited ridicule. She'd tell off-color jokes about topics that the others had long finished discussing—jokes which confused everyone, and at which no one laughed. Then she'd put on a serious face, as though she'd never meant them as jokes at all. Observing all this, Kim would at first be nervous. Then, gradually, he became displeased, but he felt totally helpless. This was how he often acted when he felt embarrassed, when he lacked confidence because of being conscious of his short stature.

She also gave him gifts constantly. It was obvious that she'd spent considerable time carefully selecting each of those ordinary, inexpensive items, so that they wouldn't feel burdensome to him. There were books he had mentioned in passing that he wanted to read, a handy wallet, and useful items for his florist shop. She carefully wrapped each of these gifts for him. But this attention paid to his needs was lost on Kim, who always unwrapped and received her gifts with utter indifference. He even gradually grew to dislike her smell. It likely came from her perfume, or shampoo, or possibly the conditioner that she used. Whatever it was, it spread like the odor of mixed flowers. The only fragrance that Kim did like could hardly be called a fragrance at all. It was a complete lack of smell. Not until he took over the florist shop did he realize that even the finest fragrance could easily become an unpleasant odor when flowers mingled their fragrances.

*

The drive south was easy for the first hundred and twenty kilometers, until he suddenly came into a congested area, where he was forced to stop. Unlike most drivers, Kim seldom listened to traffic reports on the radio and often found himself in situations like this. He had not heard the news flash, but when the person ahead of him stepped out of his car to smoke a cigarette, he informed him that the road was blocked off for several hours because of a marathon. Absolutely nothing was moving in the closed-off area. There were no runners in sight. It appeared that they had either already passed the area or dropped far behind. Kim stared blankly at the road. He remembered a sports announcer whom he'd listened to during one of these marathons. The announcer explained that marathoners usually breathe in twice when inhaling and breathe out twice when exhaling. Kim consciously tried to breathe in and out this way. The air coursed through his body and returned to the atmosphere. He'd never taken the time to notice this delicate everyday phenomenon taking place in his body, as if it were completely unimportant.

When the road reopened, he continued driving south. After some time, the cell phone in his pocket rang. It was an unfamiliar number. He suspected it was the friend who'd ordered the wreath he was delivering, and that, getting anxious, he was calling to urge him to hurry. Perhaps the elderly man had just died and the mortuary looked empty without the wreath that hadn't yet arrived. Kim didn't bother to answer the phone.

Customers were forever calling to complain about deliveries being late and insisting that their orders be delivered more quickly. So when a customer demanded to know when his order would arrive, Kim would respond: "It will certainly be there in about ten minutes." He assumed that the customer would understand that, in ten minutes, traffic and road conditions could change. If the customer called again, Kim would say he was in the vicinity and pretend he had a wrong address. The customer would then hurriedly give him the correct one.

Providing a wrong address for a deceased person was actually a mistake that did sometimes happen. Fortunately, however, there were also times when a delayed delivery didn't matter. Those were times when unexpected events occurred for either the customer or the recipient of the flowers. It might happen, for example, that a person might receive a message from a departing lover while waiting for the arrival of a bouquet that was meant to accompany a marriage proposal. The opening ceremony of a new business might suddenly be disrupted by criminals appearing on the scene. A mother might faint after delivering a stillborn baby. These were the fortunate occasions when it was of no consequence if flowers arrived late.

Driving past a tollgate as he was exiting the highway, Kim was abruptly confronted by the huge signboard of the funeral home. Below the signboard, tossing and turning in the wind, was a banner announcing its opening. The stark, square building stood in the middle of a farming area. The harvest season was over. The fields lay fallow. Kim was late, but considering the distance he'd had to travel from another city, he considered his arrival time quite acceptable. The mourners wouldn't come in flocks until late evening. As for the wreath, it wasn't the time of its arrival that was important. It was the sender's name.

Just as Kim was about to enter the funeral home's curved driveway, his phone rang again. Without slowing down, he reached for it and almost hit the guardrail. His tires squealed as he barely managed to pull onto the shoulder. His heart pounded, and the phone continued ringing as if cheering for him. It was the friend who had ordered the wreath.

"Where are you?"

"Almost there."

"At the funeral home, you mean? Come to the hospital first."

"Why?"

"He's not dead yet."

"You mean he's still alive?" he asked, then immediately realized this was an improper response. He should have responded as if it were good news that the man was still alive. However, that response would have been just as inappropriate as the other. When confronted with death, the wisest thing is to avoid lighthearted language and say nothing.

"I just asked you a question—you mean he's still alive?"

It sounded as though the friend was sighing or searching for words with which to reply. Perhaps he was restraining himself from saying anything, because telling the truth would make him appear unsympathetic. Then, to Kim's bewilderment, his friend continued to speak as though he was answering his own question even though it was the same question Kim had asked.

"He isn't going to last long. Let's go to the hospital and watch his passing together."

But instead of going to the hospital, Kim headed downtown. He wasn't hungry, but he felt the need to kill time so he entered the first noodle shop he saw. He was determined not to go to the hospital. He had no desire to see the man's death. Just as he'd never wanted to watch the moment of a bloody birth. As far as he was concerned, birth was an event in his past, and death existed only in his distant future. He wanted nothing to do with either of them at this point in his life. When the funeral started, he'd deliver the wreath, as any delivery person would be expected to do and return to his own city. On returning, he'd have to save face by compensating for lost hours and failing to fulfill his other obligations.

The atmosphere in the restaurant was leisurely since it wasn't a regular mealtime. Nevertheless, they were extremely slow coming to take his order, bringing water, and preparing and serving his food. He didn't try to hurry the owner, though. It was only forty minutes ago that he'd received the call from his friend. Time was moving so slowly. Perhaps it was also moving slowly for the elderly patient as he awaited his death. Kim considered those forty minutes. He had never before waited forty minutes for someone to die. He wondered what it meant to have one's life prolonged by forty minutes. As the deathwatch continued, his feeling of sadness lessened. He spent most of the time blankly staring out the window. If he had had several other deliveries to make in this general area, as he usually did in most places, he could have gone on to deliver those flowers and spent his time more efficiently while waiting for the funeral to start. He might have attended an opening ceremony for a new business, delivered a standing wreath of orchid blossoms, and even been given some of their red bean rice cake. He could have gone to a maternity ward to deliver a basket of flowers sent to a mother by her husband's coworkers holding her newborn whose eyes were not yet open. He could have delivered a boxed bouquet of red roses to a man who was about to propose marriage. He could have delivered a wreath to the mortuary for someone who had died earlier. But there was nothing else for him to do in this town except to keep this deathwatch. He went outside after having slowly eaten his noodles. Fifty-eight minutes had passed since receiving the call from his friend. He had still more time on his hands as he waited for the man's death.

He drove along through the small downtown and stopped in front of a grocery store that reminded him of the canned fish cakes someone had brought him from this town some time ago. Canned noodles and canned fish cakes were this town's specialties. The person who had given them to Kim thought of them as humorous gifts, and hadn't known that they were in fact emergency provisions to be used in case of a disaster.

According to old records, the town was located in the vicinity of two geological faults, and long ago had experienced a notable earthquake. This happened shortly after Kim was born, and the residents were reminded of it every time there was a need to warn them of any kind of danger. Unreinforced electric lines, water pipes, and gas lines had been destroyed. There were sporadic fires. Old wooden houses were badly shaken before completely collapsing. When the earth trembled, buildings with more solid walls quickly collapsed. Cars and people were crushed among piles of debris. Roads and bridges were damaged. Following the earthquake, strict construction regulations were enforced. All kinds of buildings were constructed to endure a certain level of earthquake. A quakeproof tunnel was built to protect all the pipes that went through the town so that delivery of electricity and water could be quickly resumed in the event of a future quake. Evacuation drills were conducted for students, and to this very day maps designating safe routes out of town still sold like hotcakes. A pessimistic scientist appeared on television.

"Although we have suffered great losses, this earthquake can't be compared to the one yet to come. Indeed, the real fear is that we can't predict when or where the next one will occur," he said. His opinion differed from that of most scientists, who believed that earthquakes could be predicted by measuring certain features of the earth's movement. But this bearer of ill tidings stared directly out from the television screen and warned: "At this very moment the earth on which you are standing could split wide open."

Despite this specialist's warnings, Kim wasn't afraid. For him, the possibility of an earthquake was the same as stories of wars ceaselessly occurring in faraway places. It was like a tsunami story that brought disaster to some other country, or the story of global warming that melted some glacier. No, for him the real disasters, disasters far worse than earthquakes or tsunamis, were the occasions when the flowers in his shop faded before he could sell them, or when some miscreant threw a stone and ran away after smashing his florist shop window. He felt no fear of an earthquake or a tsunami that might at any moment devastate thousands. The misfortune he feared was the misfortune that affected only him, while the rest of the world was well and safe.

The cans of fish cake that Kim received had eight years to go until their expiration date. Out of curiosity he had tasted one of them and discovered the liquid was salty and the fish cake swollen to the shape of a tennis ball. It tasted so awful that no one would ever be tempted to eat it except in an emergency. These days, it was said that after an emergency, food could be supplied to isolated areas within two days. So this leather-like fish cake was what people would have to survive on for two days.

Kim asked the owner of this grocery store for canned fish cakes or canned noodles. The owner, whose eyes were focused on a television program, responded briefly that they didn't have any such a thing in the store. Kim explained that somebody brought him a gift of them from this town. The owner firmly replied that they had never seen such canned goods in their sixteen years of business. But seeing that Kim was unconvinced, the owner told him to look through the stock in the back of the store, where several types of canned foods were kept. Kim went back to look. Passing by several shelves, he came to the stock of cans, a variety from different regions. There were cans of whelk, tuna, jack mackerel, mackerel, chrysalis, and fruit—cans that were commonly seen everywhere. The owner came and stood beside him and told him that they didn't have canned fish cake or noodles, but they did have a variety of fast-food packages that he could purchase. Kim said nothing. He returned to his car. On the way to the funeral home, he stopped at a few more stores, but no one sold the cans of emergency provisions he was looking for.

*

He entered the dark underground parking lot of the funeral home and carefully parked his truck, precisely parallel to the line drawn on the ground, exactly the way a casket would be placed. He decided to take a nap in the driver's seat, but then remembered that the cargo bed was almost empty. Only the wreath was back there now, shimmering in the dark like a daytime moon, exuding the faint scent of chrysanthemums. Kim climbed into the cargo bed and lay down next to the floral tributes. The cold quickly penetrated his body and, lying there in the dark, he felt like a corpse waiting to be shrouded.

If the elderly patient's life continued to drag on like this, Kim wouldn't be able to keep his date with the woman tonight. The man's death presented itself to Kim as a problem of stagnant time far removed from the sad and serious business of the world. He hesitated before deciding to call the woman. Without even asking him what had happened, she assured him that she understood. She seemed too disappointed to talk. Kim explained that he was about four hundred kilometers away and not yet done with his work. In a hesitant voice, she asked when he'd be done.

"I wish I knew, but it's not for me to decide," Kim replied. The woman said nothing. She was perhaps hurt by his curt reply, and Kim was annoyed that, as usual, he had to be so cautious about his responses to her trivial questions. Nevertheless, he repeated that his work wasn't yet finished, and he didn't know when it would be. The woman began to talk about other matters, as if she hadn't been affected at all. As their conversation continued, Kim became anxious about the possibility of receiving a call from his friend announcing the elderly man's death.

"Are you listening?" the woman asked.

"Yes, I am," he halfheartedly answered. She continued to talk, and he started to listen. She was upset about the untidy attire of a customer who visited the Customer Relations Office. It seemed she had been telling this story all along. She complained with angry sighs that the customer had demanded a refund for underwear that had been worn several times. She sounded tired. Her sighs made Kim remember how she had helped him through difficult times, but for whatever reason he suddenly felt he could no longer endure this. Although he still received comfort and warmth from her, he was convinced these feelings would not last much longer, that they'd quickly dissipate. He felt foolish for not having acted on the decision he'd already made. For some time now, he'd merely been keeping his distance, but now, listening to her complain, he felt edgy and wanted to remove himself even further from her. She stopped talking. Or perhaps she'd been silent the whole time Kim's thoughts were traveling elsewhere.

"Did you hear me?" she asked again. This time Kim honestly answered no, he had not. She sighed again, another long sigh. Merely wanting to end the conversation, Kim promised that he'd come to her house when he returned to the city. He made this promise only to comfort her because she'd been left disappointed on other such occasions. He knew if he hung up on her without promising her this, she'd again be sad, uncertain, and confused for a long time before phoning him again. Delighted with his response, she asked what time he'd be by. He replied that it would be about four hours after a man had died. Then for the first time during their conversation she burst out laughing. Evidently, she thought this was a joke.

When their phone conversation was over, Kim made his way upstairs to the funeral home. There were thirteen parlors spread out over four floors. All but one of them was empty. In this first floor parlor, the portrait of a deceased person had been placed on a marble alter. Without a chief mourner, guest mourners, fruits, flowers, or incense, the lone portrait looked strangely out of place. It was as if one of the impetuous bereaved had set the portrait there before the man had passed away. The man in the portrait had neatly combed gray hair, but even though a long time had passed, Kim could tell that this wasn't the elderly man with whom he'd been acquainted. The man portrayed here had beaming, playful eyes and was smiling slightly, as if he thought it mildly interesting to be early for his own funeral, waiting to greet the mourners even before he passed away. This lone person in the portrait in this otherwise empty funeral parlor reminded Kim of himself. Yet he was alive, and the person in the portrait was dead or about to die. Kim realized that he'd never thought seriously about death. He was living. He didn't want to think about death. Not yet. Not until the time came, far, far off in the future.

Darkness was slowly descending. The elderly man's life was slowly ebbing away. Kim stood in front of the funeral home looking at the desolate farm field as it gradually dissolved into the shadow of darkness. A man in a black suit approached him and asked for a light for his cigarette. Since the funeral home was empty, Kim guessed that this man was also dutifully waiting for someone's death. He didn't know that this man, who was wearing a badly creased black suit, black tie, and a shirt spotted with red food stains, had come to the same conclusion about him.

"My uniform got stained again. I had to work today before coming here. They gave me spicy beef stew despite my strong objections. You know, I've been fed that stew day after day, over and over again," he explained, conscious of Kim staring at the stains on his shirt. A slight smile started to appear on Kim's face when he heard the word "uniform," but it disappeared when he vaguely remembered seeing a car from the Mutual Aid Company.

"Where are you from?" the man asked, and Kim replied that he was from the florist. The man asked if the person was still not dead. Bewildered, Kim nodded his head. The man in the black suit smiled. He understood Kim's situation.

"I am in the same predicament," he said. "Could it be the same person we're waiting for?"

Wishing to avoid any further conversation with the man from the Mutual Aid Company, or more to the point, wishing to avoid any further conversation about waiting for someone to die, Kim decided to take a walk. But he took a longer walk than he intended and went all the way from the funeral home to the state highway. He still hadn't received a call from his friend. Now, standing by the state highway, he looked back toward the funeral home. Mindlessly staring at the huge, lit-up signboard, he heard himself murmur: "It seems he's still not dead." Surprised by his own unfeeling words, he fell silent.

At that instant his phone rang. If it had been his friend calling, Kim would have felt responsible for causing the elderly man's death.

"You're still not finished?" It was the woman's voice. Kim felt both relieved and anxious. His anxiety made him realize again how much distance there was between them. He knew that from now on there would be fewer conversations. Their times together, which were even now so infrequent, would become more and more inane. The tone of their voices would become less and less friendly, and they'd find fewer and fewer things to laugh about together. And all the while the woman would call more and more often, trying to understand Kim's negligence and indifference. There would come a time when she'd explode with anger, and then be overwhelmed with regret and loneliness. Then she'd apologize for having been angry. When more time had passed, and she'd repeated this scenario several times over, she would start to regret not winning his heart in return. She'd continue to waste her time wallowing in resentment and hatred. Finally, she'd realize that she didn't love Kim enough to go on any longer, or perhaps she'd decide that she hadn't really loved him to begin with. Then she'd feel empty and relieved. Kim could think of nothing to do except wait for that moment. Then, at last, he might feel something like a deep affection for her.

He lowered his voice and said: "If you push me, I will have to pray for the elderly man to die quickly." She laughed, and that made Kim nervous again. He feared it would take too long for her to sense the truth in his heart. He blurted out the word, "Enough," interrupting her laughter.

"What do you mean?" the woman asked. Kim's first inclination was to say: "That's enough joking." But it didn't feel right to him to say goodbye in that dark field where the only light came from the signboard of a funeral home. Besides, although he'd been thinking of it for some time, he still wasn't sure if he was now being impulsive and superficial. He feared he might be in his current state of mind because he was exhausted from the long, four-hundred-kilometer trip southward and this interminable waiting.

"What do you mean by 'enough'?" the woman asked again.

"Us. Us being together," he replied, under her persistent pressure.

She paused for a moment, then said: "My team manager is looking for me, I must go. Please drive carefully on your way back. I will pray for the man to die quickly."

She hung up. His heart felt suddenly heavy and not at all free, as he had thought it would.

The end of the state highway disappeared into the darkness. Kim squatted there at the side of the road with a cigarette in his mouth. A large car passed by, shaking the surface of the earth, leaving a gust of wind, and trailing black smoke. Then the road was calm again. Having chain-smoked three cigarettes, Kim was about to stand up, when he noticed something in the distance. A small white dot was approaching him and growing larger. As it drew closer, it assumed the form of white sportswear. It was a marathon runner with numbers on his shirt. As he passed by, Kim clearly heard the sound of his breathing. It was a *hu hu, ha ha*, inhaling and exhaling in even intervals through his mouth and nose. Kim watched as, little by little, he entered the obscuring darkness of the highway. The shifting white dot grew smaller and smaller until it completely vanished from sight. Weirdly, its extinction gave Kim a sudden insight. It occurred to him that the road continued beyond the dark place where it became invisible. As though in a trance, he moved toward the darkness that had so completely enveloped the white dot.

Walking on a little further, he heard the low sound of a whistle behind him. He stopped. A truck appeared out of the darkness, the same model as his own. Strangely, there was no sound of wind or wheels, no rattling of anything in the cargo bed. He thought he might have somehow missed hearing these sounds, but then again he heard the passing truck give off a clear whistle. It seemed that the driver, hidden in the darkness, was whistling. Kim stared vacantly at the truck. Then, as though startled by Kim's gaze, the truck accelerated, rounded a bend in the road, and slid along the surface. A moment later, it hit the guardrail and flipped over. Before Kim had time to react or express his shock, the truck burst into flames. The driver was nowhere to be seen. It was impossible to tell whether he'd been lucky enough to escape or if the fire had already devoured him. The flames engulfed the truck, lighting up the state highway.

Kim stood there transfixed. Then he reached for his mobile phone. But instead of calling the police, the paramedic, or the emergency room, he called the woman. She didn't answer. She might have been busy listening to a customer's complaints, or perhaps she was just angry. Kim stared at the flames. He let the phone go on ringing. After some time, the woman picked up the phone but remained silent. The sound of her shallow breathing reached his ears. It was a calm, rhythmic sound that calmed him. He imitated it, inhaling and exhaling, breathing faster than usual to keep up with her.

Then, after several attempts and still finding it difficult, he abruptly confessed his love for her. The woman remained silent. He feared this silence of hers, but he also feared what she might say if she spoke. He continued talking, frantically thinking of things to say so as not to give her a chance to respond. He spoke of the joy he experienced when he stared at her, the strange, unreal feeling he had when he held her hand for the first time, her soft breathing that was so calming for him. He spoke of his fear of not winning her love and the thrilling moment he experienced when he realized she loved him. He was saying things to her that he'd never thought about before. He was hearing his own words, but he felt they were words he'd heard someone else speak or words that he'd read. They were too conventional, too banal for him to believe they were true, but then again that was exactly why they sounded true.

He didn't understand why he was talking this way. Maybe it was because he was standing there alone on the state highway with only the funeral home signboard and the flames illuminating the area around him. The signboard was so brightly lit up it was visible from a long distance, like a beacon shining in the dark for the whole town to see. Maybe it was because he was here in this town where the students regularly drilled in preparation for an earthquake and the residents kept maps like amulets to help them return safely to their homes after a quake had struck. Maybe it was because he was in this town where canned noodles and fish cakes were sold at stores unbeknownst even to the storekeepers who'd been running their businesses for years and years. Or maybe it was because of some elderly man on the verge of death but not yet dying. If Kim had been at home, with no such problems or fears, he'd have gone on being unkind to this woman. If by some chance he'd treated her warmly, he'd have panicked, afraid that she'd misunderstand him.

Now the woman spoke. She asked him what had happened. It was such an ordinary question that Kim had no idea if his confession of love had made her happy, excited, displeased, or angry. Kim was like a stranger to himself as he spoke these words to her. Yet, because he had this feeling, he thought his confession might have some truth in it.

Regardless of the truth—regardless of her feelings—Kim knew without a doubt that he would soon be ashamed of the confession that providential fear had forced him to make. He would be angry because nothing he had said could now be taken back. He couldn't change the situation or the feelings his confession had caused. No more than he could fathom what had caused the emotions that rose up inside him. Lost in these thoughts, he hung up the phone. He thought she might call back. If she did, he wondered if he should answer. But she didn't call. The truck continued to blaze, and Kim stood motionless, silently watching the brilliant conflagration burn like a bright lantern in a funeral parlor.

MONOTONOUS LUNCH

THE SAME THING for lunch every day. Every day he ate the same thing, the Set A menu from the cafeteria in the School of Liberal Arts. And the Set A menu was always the same. It included rice, soup, kimchi and three side dishes. The three side dishes did consist of something different each day, but the overall menu was so similar from one day to the next that by the time he was on his way home, he could barely remember what side dishes he'd eaten. Likewise, he could hardly remember what he scarfed down for breakfast before leaving home in the mornings. Even the side dishes he did manage to remember confused him, as he couldn't recall whether they were from the meal he'd eaten that day or the day before. For all he knew, they could even have been on the following day's menu prominently posted on the cafeteria wall.

He filled his tray with white rice, beef radish soup, large cucumber chunks mixed with raw onions, fatty pork stir-fry and seasoned eggplant. Then, as usual, he took a table behind a post, sitting with his back to the entryway so he wouldn't have to be bothered saying hello if someone he knew came into the cafeteria. He took a sip of water from a stainless steel cup and slowly began to eat. He was so used to eating alone that he didn't look around nervously or rudely stare at anyone. Occasionally, he stared blankly into space, but for the most part he kept his eyes fixed on his tray and ate in silence.

While eating the same food at the same place at the same time each day, he wondered why he bothered to open the copy-room door on time. Might the cafeteria lunch that he ate so regularly be influencing him in this? The unappetizing crumbly rice cooked in a huge steamer, the lukewarm soup that was too salty or watery, the fatty stir-fried pork, the cold broiled fish? Perhaps it was eating the same meal every day that also deceived him into thinking that today was the same as yesterday, and that tomorrow night would be no different than tonight. Perhaps it prevented him from realizing that days and nights were passing differently for other people, while he was shut away in his base-ment copy room. His daily life was exactly like the Set A menu that, with a few small changes, was basically, perpetually the same. It consisted of always rising at the same time, dressing in the same blue or black outfits, taking the same commuter rail every morning and evening, and working the same regular busi-ness hours in his copy room.

During the previous semester, he'd made a habit of eating at the cafeteria in the School of Liberal Arts. But there were a few days when repairs were being made, and he had to eat at the nearby cafeteria in the School of Business. This cafeteria was run by a commercial company, and its reputation for a varied menu and tasty food attracted many of the professors and stu-dents. Each table was decorated with a vase containing a long-stemmed rose, and the tables were covered with neatly ironed, crisp, clean white tablecloths. Although crowded with people, the atmosphere was orderly, pleasantly quiet, and sociable. He stood in front of the large, elaborate menu board, which looked like a train schedule in Seoul Station and, after some hesitation, chose simple menu items such as a rice-and-omelet dish or kim-chi stir-fried rice.

However, after eating several meals at the School of Business cafeteria, he began to experience stomachaches in the afternoons. He was left with only one other choice for lunch—the *kimbap*[3] rolls sold by a vendor in front of the school. He disliked the taste and had no appetite at all for them, but nevertheless he unwrapped them from the foil and ate them one by one until he finished both rows in the package. He closed the copy-room door and ate them right there, ignoring the customers that constantly came by. Some customers got almost hysterical trying to turn the doorknob. Some tapped softly at the door twice as they would at a bathroom door. Not thinking, he almost knocked back to them before listlessly dropping his arm. Others knocked, and then, as if they were salespersons, called out: "Are you in, sir?" And some, knowing that he was in, pounded wildly or actually kicked the door. But no matter how urgent they sounded, he refused to open up until his lunch hour was over, at exactly one o'clock. Then he'd unlock the door, and there would be no one there. It was as though everything he'd just heard had been no more than a fantasy, and now he was left alone to wait.

Today, back at the cafeteria in the School of Liberal Arts, put-ting the last morsel of rice into his mouth, he realized that a man sitting diagonally across from his table was staring at him. The man seemed familiar to him, but perhaps it just seemed that way because he'd been staring at him for some time. He couldn't think who he was. Possibly he was one of the lecturers who frequently used the copy room. There were countless lectur-ers, though. He bowed slightly to the man, wishing to be polite rather than make a mistake and be considered rude. The man nodded back. He finished his meal and scraped his leftovers into

3 Rice wrapped in seaweed

his soup bowl for easy disposal. He stood up and glanced again at the man, whom he now noticed was eating in exactly the same way he had been eating, with his eyes firmly focused on his tray.

Walking toward the rack to deposit his dishes to be washed, he tried to figure out where he had seen this man before. Had he come into the copy room with books or materials? Was he someone he had seen urinating at a public toilet or perhaps someone in a bus or the metro who'd fallen asleep and leaned on his shoulder? Was he a man he'd seen standing at the crosswalk in front of the school gate, or a man naked in the public bath with only a towel around his neck? He considered all of these possibilities, but none rang true. As he left the cafeteria, he looked back and saw that the man was still sitting there with his expressionless face, chewing his food. Then he recalled a face, a face that was hidden behind a newspaper, and he remembered where he had seen this man before.

Following the same daily routine, it was inevitable that he had become familiar with strangers' faces. On his way to the subway station every morning, he saw a short heavy lady. She always wore high heels, which he thought was the reason she gradually fell behind him, even though she'd started out walking in front of him. All he could ever see was her back, and this concerned him, since it meant he wouldn't be able to recognize her if he were to see her in profile. At the entrance to the subway station, he saw a woman who wore a hat and handed out free newspapers. Although he'd never accepted a paper from her, she always tried to hand him one. Another familiar face was that of the woman vendor in front of the school gate, who held up a *kimbap* roll like a dumbbell and shouted to passersby that her *kimbap* was homemade and fresh. And then there was the man whose face he knew because they both rode the same commuter rail, at the same time, day after day.

He always took the train that arrived at thirty-eight past eight o'clock so that he could open the copy-room door at precisely nine thirty. He always rode in car number two. It was a little farther away from the entrance and exit, but it was less crowded. He arrived at the station early enough to read for a few moments before the message was posted on the electronic board announcing that the train had just left the nearest station. As he turned his head in the direction of the incoming train, he'd always see this man standing about one meter away from him, reading a newspaper that he held wide open. The train would appear through the black opening and approach the platform. As the train doors opened, he'd step to the left and the other man would step to the right. It was as though they were making space for a rush of water to pass between them, and the exiting passengers poured through this ravine.

It was the same as usual this morning. He and the man stood side by side in exactly the same place on the platform from which they would enter the third door of car number two. The man read the free newspaper distributed at the station entrance, while he read a textbook that he had bound for one of the lecturers. Because original texts were so expensive, and out-of-print books were not easy to find in bookstores, the lecturers often assembled and edited excerpts they collected from various sources and brought them to him to copy and bind to be used as classroom texts. The number of students expected to take a given course determined the number of books to be bound, but there were usually two or three that remained unsold, either because the students were late to drop the course or they managed to get through the whole semester without the text.

After all the students had purchased these textbooks, he simply laid claim to the unsold copies. Thus the books that populated his bookshelves were of varied content and from different fields of study. They did look similar to each other, however, since their covers were all the same color. Regardless of whether they suited his taste or not, these were the only books he read. Nor did it matter to him which one he read, since he read each one only until the next one became available. During the semester, he could read about half of each book, but at the beginning of each semester there were so many coming his way that he barely finished the first page of each one before the next one appeared.

The book he'd just started to read was an edited collection of scenes from performance art pieces. A lecturer from the School of Liberal Arts had left him the material for making the bound copies, and possibly because it was too expensive or because several students had dropped the course, six books remained unsold. He returned the book he'd been reading to a lower shelf and began to read this new one. Bodies were used quite indiscriminately in this book. The artist even used his own body— painting it with various colors to be stamped on canvas. To Kim's eyes, this creative work looked quite primitive. Frequently the performances involved bodies being injured with metal plates or exposed to some sort of violence. But regardless of the artistic purposes behind the performances, he found that he liked the artists' method of using bodies. The body was simply used as a medium or a tool for expression. It wasn't a noble object to be respected. It was either an object to be insulted and threatened or a medium through which to convey messages. He looked at these images of the body being damaged in so many different ways, and felt consoled by the sight of the artist's body, which was as unattractive as his own.

He stopped reading and thought about his own body as he had seen it reflected in the mirror. His protruding belly, his hairy forearms that no woman would ever want to touch, his short thick neck, and the brown blemishes that remained on his face from adolescent acne. He'd gained weight, so that the original shape of his face was almost completely obliterated. He'd suddenly begun to gain weight when he started working in the copy room because it required so little physical movement. He rose from his chair when a customer came in, walked to the counter, took the material, pushed a button on the machine to designate the number of copies, pushed a green button to start the copying. When the bright light flashed, he averted his eyes to look at the empty wall, the bookshelf, or the alley. He handed over the copied material, usually received paper money in payment, fumbled in the can for change, and sat back down in his chair. He repeated this sequence dozens of times a day.

When he heard the signal announcing the train's imminent arrival, he was studying another photo, under the title "A Year Spent Tied Together at the Waist."[4] It showed two people standing, facing each other, tied together by a two-meter-long rope. They'd spent a year like this, presumably so that neither one of them would be alone. All their conversations were recorded, and all the scenes of their daily life were photographed. With his attention focused on the photo, he heedlessly stepped backward and bumped into the person standing behind him. He nodded his head in apology.

He had fallen in love a few times during his school days, but that was the extent of his experience. He vaguely longed for an intimate relationship, believing that sharing lasting love and affection with another person would be like two streams of water from separate places joining to become one and flowing together. Their individual secrets would be left in the past, and they'd become like twins who were born at almost the same time.

But he was spending his whole life among students and lecturers. They were strangers with whom he had no connection

---

4 A work cited from Tracy Warr's "The Artist's Body"

and therefore no occasion, no opportunity to socialize. He had no one with whom to share opinions, no one with whom to converse or argue. He spent most of his days speaking only to students and lecturers, asking them how many copies they required or which page they wanted copied. And although he was always there in the basement copy room, few people ever remembered his face. They looked at him in the same way he looked at others, thinking only that perhaps he might have seen them somewhere. Sitting in his chair looking out at the corridor through the open door, he often smiled. But soon afterwards his face hardened as he wondered why he had. The air in the copy room was always chilly, even in summer, and the only warmth he ever felt was the radiant light the copy machine emitted when he pressed the green button. At times he stared at that light until his eyes ached and his tears flowed. The tears dried quickly.

The two people who had been tied together for a year of performance had become so terribly hostile to each other that they could solve their problems only with the intervention of friends. The abusive language they hurled at each other during that period made it clear that, if the rope weren't cut, they'd curse each other for the rest of their lives. After reading this, he closed the book, concluding that perfect intimacy with another person existed only in the longing for it, and that a distance of more than two meters was required for humans to coexist. He thought of the two-meter distance between the counter of the copy room and the corridor where the students and lecturers passed by. He maintained that distance. It was also the width of the counter that separated him from his customers. No one ever crossed to his side of the counter.

He turned his head at the sound of the train entering the station and caught another man's eye. The man gazed at him for a moment, then averted his eyes to look at the train. The noise of the oncoming train diminished little by little as it eased into the station. Then suddenly a heavy thud shattered the quiet. A man had thrown himself under the train. People screamed. For a moment he wasn't sure if he'd actually heard the thud. He thought he might have imagined it.

The train, emitting a strange sound, moved on a short distance and stopped. Chaos ensued. People who were standing on the platform edged closer to the scene. Passengers in the train peered out of the windows. With a look of horror on his face, the locomotive engineer scurried down to the tracks. Several station employees rushed down the stairs. At a station employee's command, the train doors opened. Immediately, the waiting passengers spilled out, pushing against him as he stood there motionless in their way. They moved toward the edge of the platform and shrank back in fear, finding it difficult to believe that a man had just killed himself in this place where they waited for the commuter train day after day. In obvious discomfort, they stared at the track. The station employees and firefighters who'd rushed to the scene tried to lift the empty train. When that didn't work, someone suggested that the train be put in reverse. As it moved backward, crushing the body once more, screams of grief rose from the onlookers, and the high-pitched shriek of the train's wheels resonated ominously through the station.

Drawn on by the sound, he moved closer to the rails. The sight of the body was horrible. Mangled and bleeding, it merged with pre-existing stains and darkened the crossties.

He felt nauseous but managed to step away from the scene. Thinking back, he wondered if he'd turned his head toward the man in order to witness his leap to death. Or perhaps the man had been waiting for someone to witness his death-leap. In any case, the man didn't leave a message for him. The only message, if there was one, was that of fear which now took the form of trembling and unbearable pain. Shaken, he sank down onto a bench. He checked his watch as a matter of habit. By this time he should have passed at least nine stations. He was late, and nothing could remedy the situation. The train couldn't keep to its normal schedule now. He looked around helplessly and caught the eye of another man who was holding a newspaper. He felt embarrassed and turned away, but the man came closer to him and sat down. Seated there as they were at opposite ends of the bench, it was as though they were on a seesaw.

In a trembling voice the other man said, "I've just read this article. It says that in this city, the average daily birth rate is 274 and the death rate is 106. This is the first time that one of the 106 deaths has taken place in front of me." The man dropped the newspaper. Somebody, passing hurriedly in front of them, kicked it. He picked up the paper and was about to give it back to the man, when a policeman approached.

"Sir, you were at the scene of the accident, weren't you?" He nodded. "Then you are able to act in the capacity of a reference witness and are obliged to come with us," the policeman said.

"No, I can't. I have a very important job to do today. I can't be late for it," he said shaking his head. Almost pleading, the policeman again requested that he accompany him. He answered that he couldn't cancel his appointment and that he could be questioned right there if it were necessary. The policeman then spoke in a somewhat more threatening tone.

"In the case of a death-leap, you might possibly be considered suspicious because you were standing near the victim." Once more, despite the fact that it was blatantly untrue, he asserted that his work this morning was very important. Actually the only important item on his agenda for the day was eating lunch at the campus cafeteria at noon. The policeman finally assented and let him go after obtaining his identification and contact number.

He'd have waited to see the body being removed if he hadn't been so concerned about being late for work. He hurried out of the station and hailed a cab. He told the driver that he had to be on time no matter what it might take. Then as he was sitting there in the taxi he realized he was still holding the newspaper. The taxi took off, racing over the shadows of tall buildings along the city street. It was the first time he had ever missed the eight thirty-eight train. It was going to be the first time he wouldn't open the copy-room door precisely on time. He fanned himself with the badly creased newspaper but couldn't dry his sweat. The taxi fee was going to be as much as a whole month's train fare, but even paying this large sum would not get him there on time. It was rush hour and the taxi had to take the arterial highway that was always crowded with traffic.

His heart was pounding as he frantically opened the door of the copy room thirty minutes later than usual. The rest of the world, however, remained calmly unaware of his being late for the first time in his life. Classes had already started and hardly anyone passed by. For no particular reason, he peeked out of the door and wandered out into the corridor. Time passed.

Someone came to make copies. It wasn't an urgent order. Now and then he made more copies; he sold some A4 size paper, received bookbinding requests, repaired the copy machine and sold some bound books. Finally, although he wasn't hungry, he went to the cafeteria and ate his usual Set A lunch. Because it was noon.

Returning from lunch he turned on the computer to watch a film he had saved. He kept the volume as low as possible because students could come into the copy room at any time. Some of the films had many scenes of lovemaking and others had only a

few, but he felt he had to behave circumspectly in the presence
of the students so as not to encourage strange rumors about
himself. It was two years earlier that he had started to watch,
one by one, the films listed in a book entitled, *The 1001 Movies
to See Before You Die*. A male student had brought the material
to him and allowed him to bind two copies after he claimed
that it wasn't possible to bind only one. The student never came
back to pick them up, and he couldn't remember the student's
name. He browsed the book quickly, stopping to read detailed
descriptions when he came across enticing titles or photos. It
was then that he realized he had never made a list of things to
do before he died. He suddenly became aware of the cold air of
the basement copy room and knew he'd spend his entire future
there. He would from time to time get a paper cut, and that was
the only kind of scar he'd ever have. In the warmth of the copy
machine's radiant light, he'd find comfort in this scar, and he'd
always, quite precisely, make change with nickels and pennies.

Although he didn't have a pleasing appearance, he had never
experienced a long-term illness. The toner and the dust from the
paper often made him congested and gave him a sore throat, but
with a few pills these discomforts could be borne. He still had a
good immune system and could be considered a healthy person.
Consequently, he decided to think about making a list of things
to do before dying. It occurred to him that organizing such a
to-do list might make him want to live longer, but he was unable
to think of enough things to make a very long list. Just then two
students came in to make copies. He took their material, set the
machine to copy and pressed the green button. The radiant light
slipped out and shone on his face. One of the students saw the
cover of the book he had been reading and had left open face
down. Pointing at the title, the student said to his friend, "1001

films! Watching all of those would kill you. Only someone who wanted to die would watch all of them."

He laughed to himself. He thought it wouldn't be all that bad to do nothing but watch these movies until he died. It wasn't that he was really fond of watching films. He watched the weekend movies on television sometimes, but few of the ones he'd watched so far were mentioned in the book. As he handed the copied material to the students, he decided that he'd watch the films listed in the book one by one until he died. He imagined dying while sitting in a chair or lying in bed watching a movie.

Both of his parents had died in accidents far from their home. His father, who enjoyed mountain climbing, dared a steep slope to reach an unknown medicinal herb and fell to his death. His hiking companion later explained that the plant his father had tried to pick turned out to be just a bellflower root rather than a medicinal herb. His mother died in a highway accident. She and her sister were on their way back from visiting his father's grave, when their car suddenly stopped in the middle of the road. Other cars were rushing by at dangerous speeds. His mother switched on her emergency light and with difficulty managed to pull over onto the shoulder where they felt safe and grateful to be alive. But while they were waiting for the insurance man to arrive, his mother impatiently lifted the hood of the car. "It looks so complicated," she might have said, peering down at the dark mass of machinery. "No, you know it can't be as complicated as the human mind," his aunt might have responded. They had often shared sentiments such as these when viewing mechanical objects, but this time his mother didn't hear what his aunt said. She was just about to lift her head, when a truck driver, who was trying to overtake the car ahead of him, ran onto the shoulder and hit her.

After his parents' death, he took over their copying business. He had no other choice, as he had not done anything in particular after finishing school. Now on weekends he did little else besides visiting his parents' gravesite. He swept the dirt off the tombstones and weeded here and there. The gravesite was located midway up a mountain. He had heard that a good mineral spring could be found on the way up to the peak from the grave site, but he never climbed up to find it. He knew very little about medicinal herbs, but even if he had been given the necessary information he wouldn't have dared to climb the mountain to pick them. Western medicine worked quite well for him, whatever his symptoms might be. He also took his car in for regular checkups and immediately dealt with any minor problem that occurred. While driving on the highway he attentively kept to the speed limit and never ventured onto the shoulder.

It was a comforting pleasure to cross films off the list one at a time. Some films touched his heart in spite of negative comments describing them as tedious or difficult to understand. Some films were so dull, they bored him out of his mind. Nevertheless, he watched every one of them to the very end. He watched them in his spare time during working hours and at home lying on his sofa gradually dozing off. This lifestyle wasn't at all onerous for him.

He had just started to watch a new film that was in black and white with very little dialogue. The action was so slow-moving that he was barely aware of scene changes or the actors' expressions. He was unbearably bored and beginning to doze off, when he heard someone call him.

Piles of material to be copied lay on the counter. Embarrassed, he rose quickly.

"I noticed you're watching a film," the lecturer said, and this time he recognized him immediately. This time he knew it was the man who took the same train with him each morning, the same man he'd seen in the campus cafeteria. The material to be copied was densely covered with writing and looked like it was going to be distributed in a class that was just underway. Usually, lecturers sent students to run this type of errand, but this lecturer had come himself.

Slowly regaining wakefulness, he pressed the green button, stood silently in front of the copy machine, and let the radiant light brighten his face.

"Did the police call you?" the man asked loudly enough to be heard over the noise of the copy machine. He turned around to look at the man whose sweat-dampened hair clung to his forehead, and who looked tired standing there in his crumpled blue suit.

"No, I didn't receive any call," he replied.

"I receive their calls continuously. They want me to be a witness to assist them in their investigation. These frequent calls from the police could make my assistant suspicious of me," the lecturer said.

"You could disconnect your phone."

"But then the police might come looking for me at the school. I can't let that happen. The professors would imagine all sorts of strange things about me."

"I don't think the police will do that to you. After all, we didn't push the guy."

"You're right. We didn't push him," the lecturer despondently repeated.

He nodded silently in response, and then suddenly remembered the crumpled newspaper. He had brought it all the way back to the copy room, but now had no idea where he'd put it. He turned, looking for the newspaper, and accidentally pressed the green button. Hurriedly he reached for the cancel button, but again he pressed the wrong one and ended up with an incorrect number of copies. It was the first time he'd ever made such a mistake.

He pulled out the last batch of copies, determined which ones were extra, discarded them, and restarted the machine to continue making the rest of the copies. The machine steadily spewed out paper. The blue light leaked through the thin gap between the glass and the cover, brightening his face, and he remembered having heard that when a person died, the remaining light slipped out of his body. Although he hadn't noticed it, there must have been a light lingering for a long time at the station this morning.

That evening, when he was about to leave the train station, he turned and walked instead to the opposite exit and proceeded down to the platform where he usually took the eight thirty-eight morning train. He stood in the usual place where he waited for car number two. It was six fifty-eight, exactly ten hours and twenty minutes since his departure from there this morning. Ten hours and twenty minutes. He repeated the numbers as though he never wanted to forget them. He thought about what he had done during that period of time. He'd hurried to open the copy-room door, bound several books, sold bound books, made copies of some parts of books and materials, repeatedly cleared the machine of jammed paper, and at noon he ate the Set A Lunch. Afterwards, in his spare time, he watched a film, dozed off, made copies of some pages, cleared the machine of jammed paper, sold bound books, and bound several more books. The Set A Lunch at noon had divided his day into two parts, morning and afternoon. But it wasn't only morning and afternoon that were divided in this way. Yesterday and today were divided by midnight. Last week and this week were divided by the weekend.

Last year and this year were divided by the end of the year. The future would always be divided from the past, the present divided from the past, and the future from the present. It would always be this way. Thinking this he sighed, but he also felt relieved. He stopped sighing.

There were a few people waiting for the train. They seemed to be watching the sun setting beyond the rounded arch roof of the station. He stood at a distance from the others and watched. The red-tinged sky flooded color onto the station. The crossties looked solid, like old wood, revealing sorrowful, dark energy. The signal sounded and within seconds the train roared in. The people waiting entered the train as other passengers streamed out and rushed to the exit. Passively standing there, he was easily pushed aside. The train and the passengers swept the dark red energy along with them. Only dim energy remained at the station.

He stepped closer and stared at the place on the railway track where the man had been crushed to death. At this very place, people had passed to go to work, to business appointments or company interviews soon after the detritus of the accident had been cleared away. People must also have passed over these same railway tracks to return home to their families, to visit their lovers, or perhaps to apologize for having caused some distress. Every one of them had traveled in trains whose enormous wheels had rolled over tracks that rested on these dark, bloodstained crossties, and the stains now looked like ordinary stains that had always been there. No traces of the morning remained. Ten hours ago, a man stopped breathing. His body was torn to pieces and reduced to mere stains. His remaining light now hovered unnoticed in the surrounding air. Nothing should be the same, but it appeared that everything was still the same.

When he arrived at the police station, the policeman sitting next to the entryway asked him why he was there. He hesitated. After closing the copy-room door, disconnecting all the electronic equipment, and turning off the florescent lights, his mobile phone had rung. It was an unfamiliar number, and he was unsure of what to do. Then because he remembered the lecturer saying that the police had constantly called him, he didn't answer. But if he had known that he was going to the police station this evening, he'd have answered the call and asked where the station was located. Now he hesitated before telling the policeman that he had been a witness to the morning accident.

"Morning? What accident do you mean?" the policeman asked him. "It was in the train station at thirty-eight past eight o'clock," he started to answer, but another policeman interrupted. "The death-leap. You know, at the railway station." Only then did the policeman refer him to the officer in charge of the accident, who wasn't especially welcoming either. He asked why he'd come to the station.

"I received a phone call from the police," he stuttered.

"A phone call?" the policeman repeated.

He nodded his head and with little confidence attempted to reply.

"I have to give testimony regarding the accident," he said.

The policeman looked dubious, but took him into another room.

"At this point, after everything has been settled and the body has been removed, I don't know why anyone here would have called you," the officer muttered as though he was talking to himself. He turned on the CCTV screen to look at the video that had been taken of the accident, and asked, "Look, where are you?" He looked but wasn't able to find himself on the screen.

The policeman, alternately watching him and the TV, tapped on the top part of the screen. He appeared there as a very small person. His short neck wasn't visible at all. He looked more like a folk doll than a human being, some kind of a folk doll simply consisting of two parts, a head and a body. Other people looked like goldfish in a bowl, tranquil but constantly moving. Then he saw himself moving as though he too was in a fishbowl. He thought he had been doing nothing more than quietly reading his book while waiting for the train, but now he saw that he had been reading for a few moments, looking at the railway tracks, looking in the direction of the incoming train, and looking at the electronic signboard that, minute by minute, announced the train's arrival time. He looked at his watch, at the person next to him, then stepping back he bumped into someone, apologized and returned to his reading. He had been constantly moving. Then the train roared into the station spreading its light, and almost immediately the man had jumped onto the tracks. He was well aware of the sequence of events that followed.

The policeman rewound the film. The train immediately disappeared like an actor who'd come on stage by mistake, and the people flipped backwards. Like some kind of Superman character, the dead man leaped back up onto the platform. But on returning to the platform, the dead man wasn't reading a newspaper as he'd thought. He was only holding the paper and staring vacantly in the direction of the oncoming train as if hallucinating. Then he glanced around him before leaping to the tracks and disappearing. Immediately, people on the platform crowded around, confused and frightened.

He spotted himself on screen again. This time he was bending down and getting up again. It wasn't obvious why he had done this, but he knew. He was picking up the leaper's newspaper, which had been dropped to the ground nearby him. It was badly crumpled, as though the leaper had been grasping it tightly. The police officer zoomed in, and the picture quality diminished.

"We could have saved him at just that moment," the policeman said regretfully as he tapped the screen. He had probably viewed this scene many times, for as soon as he uttered these words, the train passed over the exact place where the man had fallen. People swarmed toward car number two. The locomotive engineer and station employees panicked and ran about in confusion. Some people stared. Others were stunned and turned away.

He saw himself slipping out of the crowd. He stared at the scene for a moment and then retreated to the bench. He looked blank, but in fact he had been checking his watch, thinking about what kind of alternate transportation he might take, and organizing his thoughts as he looked at the wrinkled newspaper. There were various statistics listed in the paper under the heading: "A Look at Daily Life Through Numbers." In the city where he lived, the average daily number of births was 274, and the daily average number of deaths was 106. It was the first time one of the 106 died in front of him, he thought. While he was sitting there by himself, a policeman approached. He spoke a few words, then abruptly stood and ran up the stairway as though escaping. The screen continued to show the crowd in confusion in front of car number two. Having emerged from the screen he was now silent. The policeman stared at him. "So what do you have to say?"

"It was when he jumped…" he wet his dry lips and continued, "I picked up the newspaper he dropped."

"The newspaper?" the policeman asked as he turned off the CCTV and the screen turned black. "Please, just throw it away."

He rarely took any train other than the eight thirty-eight. When on occasion he had something to do in town, he'd always take his car or a bus. He was afraid that if he took the train, he'd end up in the copy room. But this night he made an exception. The train started out moving slowly, and he saw the reflection of his face in the window. It was a tired face, but that was true on most evenings. His heart began to beat in time to the speed of the train, slowly at first then finally pounding so strong and so rapidly that he had to press his hands against his chest. He felt that something was pulling at him. He was aware of stains, lights, sighs. He forced himself to his feet. His leg had gone to sleep. His heartbeat slowed. He felt a cramp in his foot and realized that he had just passed the crossties where the man's body had been crushed.

The basement at night was cold and damp but pleasantly cool. He opened the copy-room door and turned on all the lights. Light flooded out into the dark corridor. He went to the scrap-paper box, where he found very little waste had accumulated in the last few days. He usually produced scraps only when paper jammed in the machine, but on the afternoon when he made copies for the lecturer, extra pages had been discarded because of his mistake. Now, as he searched the box, he couldn't find these pages. His only clue was that he remembered they were filled with writing, but of course that was true of almost all the scrap paper. "We didn't push him, did we?" The lecturer's words resonated in his ears, and he remembered the lecturer's tired face. He found the newspaper at the bottom of the scrap-paper box. It was badly wrinkled. He threw it back into the box and locked the copy-room door from the inside. He heard the wind from the corridor hitting the door. It sounded as though someone was knocking quite loudly. He was sure it was the wind, but a few times as he looked at the closed iron door, it seemed to him that it was feigning ignorance.

"Is anyone out there?" he shouted, but no one answered.

After staying up all night, he opened the copy-room door at the regular hour. From time to time students came in, and he made copies for them. He sold bound books, he heard complaints about the high price of bound books, and he smiled slightly as he handed them their change. It had been some time since the copying machine had had maintenance service. It was making black stripes on the copies. So he took some time to repair it. His mother had said that machines were complicated, but his aunt said they were not as complicated as the human mind. He was able to repair the computer. The paper and toner he had ordered arrived. He checked to make sure he had the correct number of each size of paper. He checked the toner for color and size before signing for them.

Finally it was noon. He wasn't hungry, but he went to the cafeteria in the School of Liberal Arts and bought a meal ticket. There were three kinds of side dishes besides kimchi. They were marinated seaweed, fish baked with seasonings, and vegetable noodles. He filled his tray abundantly with them. He attempted to remember what he'd eaten the day before, but to no avail. It made no difference. Today's food would be forgotten too. He carried his tray to his usual seat behind the post. He drank his water and slowly began to eat.

WOULD YOU LIKE TO TAKE A TOUR BUS?

THE SACK WAS right there in the middle of the large storage container, and the container appeared to be larger than it actually was because there was nothing else in it except for the sack.

"Is this it?" K asked as he entered the container.

"Is there anything else here?" S responded as he entered after K and the container reverberated with the tung tung sounds of their footsteps. They lifted the sack, each of them holding one end of it. It wasn't light. Actually, it was on the heavy side, and lifting it required the strength of two men, but only two men. S and K were of similar heights. Thus the weight of the sack was evenly distributed between them. In fact, it may well have been because of their similar bodies and heights that these two men were chosen for the task. Together, they could carry it easily.

"It's heavy."

"It certainly isn't light."

They didn't bother to count to three before lifting it, and they simply synchronized their steps as they exited the container, situated at one corner of the parking lot and typically used for departmental storage.

"How come this storage compartment is empty?" K asked as he closed the door.

"It's because our desks are used for storage now. Everything that used to be kept in storage compartments is now piled up on our desks," S replied.

"Even so, aren't there generally some things that are supposed to be in the storage compartments?"

"Usually yes. They keep documents there that they will never again see in their lifetimes. But for our jobs we need nothing more than telephones and paper. So I guess, there is hardly anything to be kept in storage anymore," S said as he turned the key to lock the compartment. "Actually, I really like the storage compartments to be empty." K looked at him dubiously. "The things that are in storage are usually things that will always remain there, documents and so forth that matter for nothing. They might as well be thrown away. It looks as though this empty storage space is the result of some items finally being discarded."

K thought that the way S talked was quite similar to the way their boss talked. This didn't really bother him, though. He felt it was rather normal for one person to emulate another person's speech. He wondered about his own manner of speaking, which was also sometimes similar to their boss's manner.

The sack was old fashioned and dirty. There among the gray buildings and the black cars, it closely resembled a trash bag.

"That looks like it would be good for holding rice or barley, don't you think?"

"Well, you could say that, but you don't really know because you've never packed rice or barley."

"So? How many city people can you count who've packed rice or barley?"

"Grain might spill out of this kind of a sack."

"Wait a minute," K said as he rubbed the sack with his fingers. "It's thick. It feels like it has a vinyl lining." As he continued to rub it, the sack responded with a 'suhgok suhgok' sound.

The top was tightly closed. In order to see the contents, they'd have had to cut the top open with scissors, but they knew they couldn't do this. One of their boss's orders was that it shouldn't be opened.

"I wish it was a trunk."

"Yes, that would make it much more charming to look at, and it would be easier to move because it would have wheels."

"Why didn't the boss call some expedited delivery service for this job?"

"That's what he uses us for."

"You mean we are his deliverymen?"

"Who else?"

"So when we return after this delivery, are we going to receive little stickers as rewards?"

"Usually a deliveryman gives a sticker."

"Then should we give one to our boss?" They looked at each other and shook their heads. No, their boss wasn't a person who would appreciate that kind of humor.

They left the storage area and immediately took a taxi to the bus terminal. They placed the sack, which did look somewhat similar to one in which a farmer might carry his grain, into the taxi trunk. Their instructions were to deliver it. Their boss had ordered them to carry it to a designated place, but under no circumstances were they to open it.

"That's simple enough, isn't it?" he had asked looking at K and S who sat facing each other. They nodded in unison. 'Simple, isn't it?' was a question, although it was really more of a statement, that their boss habitually asked after having provided a job description.

Next he told them to go to the terminal and take the express bus to D City. They nodded again. Their final destination was still unknown. They were told that each time it was necessary, a written message would be sent to them. This didn't seem strange. Normally, jobs were done one step at a time. They were about to leave, when their boss called them back and told them to sit down again.

"As simple as it is, will you make a mistake?" their boss asked them. He wasn't a man who indulged in humor, nor was he especially imposing. This was a serious question.

"Actually I myself am very nervous, as I am also in the position of receiving orders," he told them. If this task was one for which even their boss had to receive orders, K and S thought perhaps it might concern the president or the chairman of the company.

"Look," K later said to S, "I was given this." He took a paper out of his bag. The words, "Tour Bus Pass" were written on the upper part of it.

"When did you receive this?"

"When you went to the men's room, the boss called me and gave it to me."

S carefully examined the paper K handed him. He saw that there was no date on it and that it could be used on similar buses at any time. In small print on the back were specific directions for using it.

"This sort of thing is new to me. A Tour Bus Pass."

"It's new to me too. It reminds me that it has been a long time since I have taken a tour bus. How long ago was it for you, do you remember?" K asked.

"We don't usually take tour buses, do we? We take rental buses to go to weddings or company training tours. I don't think I have taken a tour bus since I went on field trips in school."

"Unusual, isn't it? Though I think every so often I do see tour buses on the road," K said.

"It always looks like they're used for group tours. I detest group tours. I mean, visiting some historical site or an industrial complex. That sort of tour. Those look-alike tour buses that follow each other along the road and stop at tourist spots or shopping centers. The tourists standing in lines, taking pictures, bundling themselves back into buses, bundling out again at the next tourist spot and…"

"Kind of a circular route, isn't it?" K responded.

"As long as it returns to the starting point, it is."

"By the way, why are you going to the restroom so often?"

"The truth is, I am not feeling well," S admitted. "My intestines are bothering me. When I'm nervous, I feel like my whole body turns into one big intestine."

K laughed, and S thought that he was trying to change the subject. During this exchange concerning his intestines, S wondered what else K might have received besides the tour bus pass. S could accept injustice but not disadvantage. However, he decided not to cross-examine K. He thought that one's job should be done in proportion to the amount of payment received. He asked K to keep the tour bus pass with him and got out of the taxi.

*

They stored the sack in the baggage compartment of the bus. The driver held the numbered receipt out to S, but S looked away so that K would have to take it. Displeased, K stared at S, but having no other choice, he accepted the receipt. Pretending to be unaware, S climbed onto the bus and looked for his seat number. K glanced around inside the bus and then sat down next to him. There were only a few empty seats left. The bus was just leaving, but the passengers already looked tired, as if they'd only arrived at this stop after traveling for a long time.

"Where are all these people going on a weekday?"

"Don't know. But we are certainly the only disgraceful-looking ones traveling with a sack like this!" S complained.

They dozed until the bus stopped at a rest area. They tried to remember but couldn't recall another time when they had taken a nap like that on a weekday.

"They must be holding the regular meeting by now," K said. He had returned from the restroom and was slurping fishcake soup.

"Yes. Luckily, I had nothing at all to contribute," S replied.

"Me neither." Although K said this, he was in fact rather talkative during these meetings. Sometimes he spoke for their boss. Sometimes he spoke to agree with someone else's idea, and other times to agree with a majority opinion.

A man got onto the bus and distributed numbered slips to each of the passengers. They accepted the slips without thinking. K received number 7, and S, number 8. The man explained that he was going to draw a few winners for gift watches to be given away by a company that had gone bankrupt. S looked down at his own worn-out watch strap.

"He's obviously trying to trick us into buying something," K said. S nodded. The man called out numbers. "Number 9, 15, and 7." K sprang up.

"I'll go see what scam he's promoting." K got off the bus and followed the man. Two people, who were holding the numbers 9 and 15, followed along. S fumbled with his watch while he waited. K returned shortly empty handed.

"So did you get a watch?"

"Only if I'd buy a navigation device," K laughed. "I don't even own a car." Sitting back down in his seat, K closed the pleated curtain on the window. The interior of the bus became a little darker. S took off his watch and stashed it in his pocket. They continued dozing off until they arrived at D City.

D City was located in a basin. From the terminal they could see that D City was itself a basin. Dim lines of mountains surrounded them in all directions. The city they lived in was also surrounded by mountains but, because it was in a basin, D City felt warmer.

"Have you been here before?"

"No, it's my first time."

"They say this city is famous for its raw meat."

"Raw meat?" S repeated as he looked down at the sack that rested like an inert lump between their two seats. K poked it lightly with his fingers.

"I just don't know," he said. "It feels like a bundle of paper, or something mushy, like maybe there's raw meat in it. I mean, at first I thought it felt mushy, but then it also feels hard, then again it feels mushy."

S also poked the sack here and there, exactly as K had done, and it felt, just as K had said, like a piece of wood on one side and a mushy chunk of meat on the other. As for the sack itself, it remained silent and limp as a rag doll while their fingers poked and prodded it from all angles.

They sent a message that they had arrived at D City, but their boss didn't respond. He was a busy executive who had to attend meetings, sign approvals, and keep appointments with customers. They didn't expect a quick response.

The terminal was crowded, and the chairs were too hard to be comfortable for any length of time. Squirrels climbed nearby trees. K and S walked to a conveniently close café. They read the newspaper they'd purchased before leaving the terminal. The first page featured an article about a game played by the D City professional baseball team the day before. The team wasn't one of K and S's favorites. Nonetheless, they felt it was a good thing that they had purchased the newspaper. They settled the sack under the table, divided the newspaper between them, and enjoyed a leisurely span of reading. S went off to the restroom only once.

"This is a part of our business trip, isn't it?" S asked.

"Of course it is."

"Then shouldn't we buy some gift items on our way back?"

"Yes, we should."

When their colleagues returned from their business trips, they always brought various regional specialties such as pastries with sweet red bean fillings, walnut pastries, barley pastries, and potato cakes to share with their coworkers.

"When we see something interesting on our way back, we should buy it. But we can't bring raw meat. That would be too difficult to distribute."

They went back to concentrating on their newspaper. Whenever they stretched their legs, the sack was in their way, but K finally managed to stretch his legs and avoid it. From time to time as they read, they glanced at their mobile phone. There was still no message from their boss. He was probably also waiting for a message. S became restless. He folded his section of the paper and accidentally kicked the sack as he moved his foot. Then suddenly he leaned under the table and sniffed at it.

"Don't you smell something coming from the sack?" he asked. K put his nose to the sack to smell it.

"It smells sour. Like something has gone sour," S said.

"But the odor isn't that strong. It might have come from the cargo compartment of the bus. I saw a woman in the bus put a big container in the compartment. It smelled like kimchi." There were other possible sources as well. A rusty iron smell from the storage container might have rubbed off on the sack, and anything after all could acquire a bad odor when stored for a length of time in a confined space.

Still no message arrived from their boss. S was bored. He looked around the café and realized it could have been an arboretum, there were so many flowerpots. Most of them contained tall plants with foliage that reached the ceiling. K touched one of the rubber tree leaves near him. The edge of the leaf had turned yellow even though it was artificial. Touching the plastic leaf, he suddenly realized, felt much the same as touching the sack. Startled, he was simultaneously reminded of something else.

"What if we can't finish this job today?" he asked. Only then did S realize that they had no way of knowing how long it might take them to deliver the sack. In case of a delay they might have to stay overnight in D City. They didn't know their final destination or who the recipient was. They didn't know when their boss's message would arrive. If they had to continue waiting as they were waiting now, it could take several days to make the delivery. It occurred to K that if he had known that they'd be caught in this situation, he could have searched for a clean and spacious place to stay. His heart sank, but it wasn't because of the lodging problem. He was thinking about matters that needed to be taken care of back in his office. If he didn't finish this job today, he'd lose time, and the same amount of work would be there waiting for him when he returned.

"I forgot I had to contact Mr. Murata, a Japanese customer," S said gloomily. K deduced that this could be a serious mistake. He also thought about S's habitual procrastination and wondered why he was like this. It occurred to him that S would do much better if he organized his work and dealt with it in a more timely fashion. He felt it was inevitable that S would be in difficulty with his business affairs.

"Why don't you call him now?" he suggested. S fumbled through his daybook and found Mr. Murata's phone number. He was about to call when he lost his nerve.

"It's no use. I must know the progress of the increased production cost for each of the materials. What Mr. Murata wants to know is the domestic price of raw material last month. The document that contains that information is in the office. And my relationship with him isn't such that we call each other just to say hello."

"Of course, you're right. Nothing works without the documents."

K kicked the sack and turned his head away. Like S, he also remembered work that needed to be done and was left behind. Also like S, he could find no way to tend to it now because most of the documentation he needed in order to make any progress was in the office.

Feeling depressed and finding nothing else to do, they ended up completing the crossword puzzle in the newspaper. It took quite a while for them to find a word with two syllables starting with "b" which meant an unnecessary or useless thing. Eventually they found it. S went to the restroom and returned once more. Soon afterwards, the message arrived from their boss.

"I'm sorry for the delay, but it was because I myself had to wait for a message," he explained. "From there you are to take an intercity bus and go to B County."

They sprang from their seats. Together they lifted the sack, each holding one end. S let his end go slightly slack feeling that K should shoulder more of the burden. The sack hung between them like a small child holding onto his parents' hands.

The intercity bus terminal was fairly close to the express bus terminal. But that wasn't advantageous because it was too close to take a taxi, and they were forced to walk carrying the sack all the way. Just as it became too heavy to carry any farther and they were about to take a break, they arrived at the terminal. They loaded the sack onto the bus.

"What is this?" the bus driver asked as he took their tickets.

"A sack."

"I can see that. My question is what kind of sack? What's in it?"

"Rice," S quickly improvised.

"Well, please be careful not to tear it. I don't want you to spill that grain," the bus driver admonished them, without touching the sack. Feeling relieved, they carefully laid it in the passage way next to their seats. A woman sitting across the way from them sniffed as though she smelled something unpleasant. K and S closed their eyes and pretended to be sleeping. But though they kept their eyes closed, they couldn't sleep—probably because of the coffee they had been drinking.

Later, with their eyes partly open, they talked about the previous week's business as if they were giving a weekly report. K had opened a letter of credit with a production cost three percent lower than the previous month. He said he'd discussed lowering production costs with their boss but had been unable to convince him.

S agonized because he'd exceeded the margin of error, as concerned the difference of the total weight between the imported magnesium and that quoted in a letter of credit. He reported this to his boss thinking that he could file a claim to their customer. His boss told him that instead of filing a claim to their long-term customer he'd rather amend part of the letter of credit. He also said that they should take time to think the matter over.

S and K realized that each of them had gone through some difficulty at work this past week. At this point in their conversation, they also realized that they hardly knew anything about each other except for the schools they'd attended. They'd both been hired at the same time. They could easily have had a good relationship, if they hadn't so often been thrown into an invisible arena of competition. Their boss usually lit the fire. He'd tell S that K was going to participate in some project and then say, "How about you?" Or, he'd ask K if he realized that S had submitted two proposals at a given time. Hearing remarks like this from their boss, S would feel his stomach lurch, and would follow K to join a project team that had nothing to do with his own work, and K would rack his brain to write another proposal. Neither of them was aiming to be outstanding. They simply wanted to be at least as good as the other.

As the intercity bus passed close by a small town K, who was looking out of the window, remarked that it looked just like the village he'd lived in as a child. S, observing the same scene, had a similar feeling.

"There was a noodle shop in my childhood neighborhood," K said.

"Was it a Chinese place?" S absentmindedly inquired.

"It was a shop that made and sold strands of noodles. They pressed out the strands and hung them up high like on a clothesline to dry. The noodles became somewhat dry and hard, and I ate them raw. They were tasty. They hung on those clotheslines just like the white sheets that we used to cover our blankets. My friends and I wandered around between the strands. The well-dried noodles made a sound like charrrr, the way the beads of a Chinese screen sound when they're pulled out to the side and then let go to fall back in place. Some white noodle pieces fell on the ground, and we covered them with dirt so the owner wouldn't see them. I can still remember the smell of that semi-dry flour."

"Do you still like noodles?"

"Not really. They don't taste as good as they did in my child-hood," K said.

"The neighborhood that I grew up in had a field of baby's breath."

"Baby's breath?"

"Yeah, baby's breath. I didn't know that it was called baby's breath until after I grew up. When I was young, I thought they were just weeds. I didn't know they were flowers, but when they blossomed and turned the field white, it was so pleasant. I felt like I was floating. The girls played house and served baby's breath pretending it was a rice dish."

"Do you still like baby's breath?

"Not particularly. But it's not just baby's breath. I generally don't care too much for any flowers."

K and S discovered that they had each spent their child-hoods in somewhat similar suburban areas. They discussed their experiences in high school, elementary school, and hometowns. They'd never lived in regions near each other, but they were able to share similar memories as though they'd spent their child-hoods together. Their friends, except for a few who'd moved to other cities, had continued to live in the same town until they were adults. At some point, they had both stopped eating semi-dry noodles, playing with baby's breath, and playing house with friends.

*

The intercity bus pulled away emitting a cloud of black smoke. S and K were left alone at the station. The name of the village written on the signboard of the bus stop was totally unfamiliar to them. They knew that B County wasn't the final destination for the sack. They knew they had still farther to go.

"Now where is he going to send us?"

"Who knows?"

This task of delivering a sack to a certain destination was similar to the work they'd been doing so far in that they were never informed beforehand what the next step would be.

This time they sent a message to their boss announcing their arrival before they actually set foot in B County. He didn't reply. They understood that he also had to wait to receive a message from his boss, and that would take some time. His superior was probably a busy person who also had meetings to attend, approvals to sign, and appointments to keep with customers.

Along the intercity bus route, they saw corner shops, a bus ticket booth, an electronics shop, a bakery, and so on, all in a row. They decided to eat at a fried chicken restaurant. There were no other customers, and the first thing that greeted them was the smell of the fried chicken. They placed the sack discreetly under the table. While eating, S bent to smell it again, and noted that it had greasy odor, but K couldn't really distinguish between the greasy smell of the frying chicken and that of the sack.

They finished a whole chicken and were still munching on pickled radish, when the message arrived from their boss to take a city bus and go to G Town.

"We'll arrive at the edge of the earth if they keep this up," K complained.

"Probably not at the edge of the earth. The scope is getting narrower, from city to county, to town." K nodded agreeably.

The old city bus rattled along. They sat on seats one behind the other with each of them holding onto one end of the sack so that it would not topple over. The bus was filled with old villagers and a number of their sacks. It could easily be seen that their sacks were filled with agricultural products, daily necessities, and farming tools. But the sack that K and S carried was the only one that was securely closed, the only one that contained a secret.

Getting off the bus, they saw broad fields on both sides of the bus stop. They spotted a few houses off at a great distance, and a huge zelkova tree somewhat closer to the road. They suspected that was the tree that marked the entrance to the village. There was a long wooden bench under the tree, where several elderly villagers were resting. The villagers moved over and made space for K and S, who enjoyed the breezy shade that dried their sweat.

This time it was S who sent the message to their boss. They assumed that, as previously, it would be a while before they received a reply. Cautiously, they stretched out on the bench, trying not to disturb the villagers. The wooden bench was as comfortable as their company's veranda. That outdoor veranda space, which had an emergency exit stairway, was where employees could smoke or chat with their colleagues. The building was square and made of cement, probably because the company had started out as a cement business. It looked so solid it was inconceivable that any kind of crises could ever take place inside of it. K casually tapped the sack with his toe in much the same way he'd have flicked ashes off his cigarette. The sack started to fall over. He stood and held it upright.

"What could be inside of it?"

"I'm not at all keen to know," S replied, and K closed his eyes trying to convince himself that he didn't want to know either. The odor from the sack was becoming unbearable, and they were sure that it would become even worse as time passed and it absorbed surrounding odors. They were just about to doze off, when the message arrived from their boss.

"Why did it have to come so quickly this time?" they complained, but they got up and grabbed the sack. They were told to look for a house with a village guardian pole that wasn't visible from the zelkova tree. They started out and came to more than one fork in the road where they had a difficult time trying to decide which way to go. It was a problem because they were not familiar with the geography of the area, but after a time the route became obvious to them. They followed a red clay road that was narrow and seemingly endless. Walking along, they heard a dog barking in the distance and occasionally a cow mooing. Black goats halted in the middle of a field to watch them passing by. They were startled by the flapping of hens' wings, and made unpleasantly aware of the stench of cow manure. They were annoyed by mayflies in their eyes and bothered even more by biting mosquitoes.

The sun was gradually setting as they continued their search for the house with the village guardian pole, and they began to doubt that they'd ever find it. Then, one by one, houses began to appear. Still, they weren't certain that they were correctly following their boss's directions until they finally spotted the village guardian pole he'd described. Behind the pole there was an old house. K thought it looked deserted. There were broken clay pots and abandoned pieces of furniture in the yard, and the front door had completely fallen off. They entered carrying the sack with them. In contrast to the dilapidated entrance, the room was neatly arranged, the linoleum floor was fairly clean and there were no spider webs, no peeling wallpaper.

"So are we supposed to deposit it here?"

"Well this should complete our mission." They dropped the sack and collapsed beside it.

"Let's take a break."

"Right. It's not possible to return at this hour anyway." It was growing dark outside, and they'd have had to walk a few kilometers to get to a populated village.

"Luckily it is dark," S said. K nodded. If it hadn't been dark they might have decided to return along the unfamiliar country road and travel all the way back to their company.

*

Stationed there between them as it was, the sack somehow appeared to be darker than the darkness that surrounded it. They removed their shoes. They were still aware of an odor but they could no longer determine if it was coming from the sack or from their unshod feet.

"There was a haunted house in the neighborhood where I grew up," S said after some time. He thought K was asleep, but K replied in a low voice: "Mine, too."

"Because of the rumor about the ghost no one would go near that house, but one day my friends and I got up the courage to go over there. If you were there, you would've joined us. Everybody went. I don't remember why. Perhaps we had made a wager with children from a neighboring village or something like that. Anyway, on the way to the house, one of us stumbled on a stone and cried. Then other children began to cry. We were actually afraid. But the crying didn't stop us. I don't know who went into the house first. I know it wasn't me. I was following the others from way behind. But I did go in. I was hardly breathing. It was so dark. I didn't realize until later that I had closed my eyes. As I opened them, things gradually began to reveal themselves. In that house there was…" S swallowed. "There was a clock," he continued. "A striking clock. It was an ordinary clock that might be in any house. We had one like that on the wall of the wooden porch room in our house. But in this house there was a broken clock rolling around on the floor."

"And then?"

"That was it."

"Fiddle-de-dee."

"No, the real thing is yet to come."

"Yes?"

"It was pouring rain that morning. It was pouring so hard, I remember, that the water ran down through the groove of the roof and dug a hole in the yard. The roads of that neighborhood had been covered with precast pavers. But hardly any of them remained intact. They were broken or in the process of being broken. Each one of those broken or cracked pavers was slanted in such a way that they held the morning rain. We walked really quietly so we wouldn't wake up the ghost. But despite all our effort, the pavers kept moving and we kept getting splashed by the muddy water. Either it was the kid ahead of me or the one behind me, or it was me. I rubbed the disgusting dirty water off my legs. Then I rubbed my dirty hands off on my shirt and pants. I just got dirtier and dirtier."

"Children's clothes were usually dirty." K commented.

"Yes, but originally they were clean."

"So what was so scary?"

"The pavers. I was scared of them. The more I wanted to keep myself clean, the dirtier they made me."

"By the way, do you think someone will come to pick up this sack now, at night?"

"There must be a night shift or someone on duty."

"If no one comes, let's open the sack." S said. K stared at it, not responding. It seemed as though a striking clock was ringing from inside it.

Every time they heard a dog barking somewhere or they saw the lights of a car, they sprang up, but the barking was brief, and the headlights quickly disappeared. As they gradually became accustomed to the night, they became unaware of other sounds, even the sounds of insects. Some time passed and they heard raindrops. S dozed off while listening to them and heard raindrops in his dream. He also thought he heard heavy footsteps. The footsteps moved around S and K as they slept, then they disappeared. S dreamed that it was his own footsteps and that he was nervously stamping his feet after having missed the return bus. He could have taken the next bus, but for some reason he was stamping his feet instead.

It was daylight when S opened his eyes and saw that K was still sleeping. He shook him awake. The sack was gone. With their eyes still swollen from sleep, they went outside. The night rain had made the road muddy. The guardian pole stared at them. The sack wasn't in the yard. The night-shift worker or someone on duty had probably stopped by.

"Have you ever done this kind of job before?"

"No, this is my first time with a sack. As you know, I have always dealt with ferronickel or magnesium."

"Same here. This is my first time."

"First time, but it doesn't feel so strange."

"Right, for some reason it feels familiar. And it feels as though doing this even once would still be a good experience."

"Yes, in the beginning I wasn't sure about this job, moving a sack and all. But now I think that it's rather a good thing that we've done it. We might not have done as well with something more complicated or bothersome. We have enough of that with things like ferronickel and magnesium."

"You're right. It wasn't too bad."

"So now it is all done, right?"

"Right."

"Really?"

"Well, for some reason I feel it's not finished."

"We may have this type of job again someday."

"Also, we still have to report to the boss."

They had a long walk on the muddy road to get to the bus stop. Their shoes and pants got dirty. S splashed muddy water at K, and K splashed muddy water at S.

The old villagers were sitting under the zelkova tree the same as yesterday. It was shady and breezy and their unfastened jackets fluttered in the wind. They were waiting for a bus that came every hour. Everything seemed the same as yesterday.

But everything wasn't the same. They got on the bus without the sack. While waiting for the bus, they ate noodles instead of chicken. K complained that they weren't as tasty as those from his childhood. After eating the noodles, they used paper napkins to wipe the mud stains off their shoes and their pants that had been splashed all the way up to the knees. On the city bus they didn't talk at all. They dozed off. Arriving at the express bus terminal, they found a restaurant in the vicinity and ate cow head stew. The regional food of this city didn't have a good reputation. This was especially true of eating places near the terminal, which were considered the worst of all. The stew, however, was unexpectedly delicious.

After finishing the stew, they told the teller at the ticket booth the name of the city where their company was located, and they bought two tickets. Then, when they were just about to board the express bus, K suddenly pulled the tour bus pass out of his pocket. They turned around and looked for the platform. A group of tour buses were waiting on the opposite side from the express bus terminal. One of them had its engine running and was about to leave. They ran toward it. The driver willingly opened the door for them, even though he grumbled that they should have arrived on time. They showed him the pass and took seats right behind him.

Strangely, the driver's back looked soft and hard like the sack. K almost sputtered the word, sack, but stopped himself just in time. S also looked at the driver's back, and almost said the same word before quickly closing his mouth.

As the bus began to speed up, the driver turned on a song with a distinct, repetitive rhythm. Passengers in the rear seats began to loudly sing along, and the driver jokingly announced that dancing wasn't allowed. Someone responded that they were having enough fun without dancing.

"Where is this bus going?" K asked.

"It's supposed to go to some tourist attraction," S replied after having looked around the interior of the vehicle. Then, as the driver pulled into the bus lane and speeded up, K and S began to sing along with the others, stopping only because they felt embarrassed.

"Shall we buy some souvenirs?" S asked. K nodded. Sitting side by side, they stared out the front window. The highway stretched on endlessly.

OUT FOR A WALK

THE WILD BOAR woke him. He was half asleep when he heard the animal's sudden cry. Wild snarling and snorting. Startled, he rose from his bed. Initially he thought it was a dog barking, but as he continued to listen, he realized it was a wild boar. His wife was asleep, snoring lightly, and in this he felt himself fortunate. If she'd woken up, she'd have insisted that he venture out to see what was going on. Sitting back down on the bed, he stared around the room. As his eyes gradually adjusted to the darkness, he could see the items of their daily life. There was nothing unfamiliar, until, in the dim light, two pills on the bedside table came clearly into view. His wife had forgotten to take her medication again. He gazed at her furtively as she slept. He was displeased with her forgetfulness, but even if she'd been awake, he wouldn't have said anything because she was pregnant, and extremely sensitive. He knew it was best not to speak words of accusation or complaint about her mistakes. He was careful to show no signs of irritation, to be especially attentive, and to obediently provide whatever she requested.

Yet she often cried and with seemingly little cause. She complained that he was indifferent to the pain she experienced from carrying their child. She cried while she told him of her overwhelming anxiety about her own and the baby's health. At first he felt sympathy for her. She wasn't the type of person who often complained or pretended that she was in pain. She'd been suffering with morning sickness throughout her pregnancy and had become much thinner. Although he too worried about his wife's health, he didn't know what he could do except give her her pills on time and try not to aggravate her sensitive nerves. They were expecting the baby soon. There were only twenty days until the due date. As the time approached, his wife complained more frequently about her pain. At first, he hadn't been enthusiastic about having a baby. However, when he found out about his wife's pregnancy, he was truly happy. He accompanied her to see the ultrasound and, even though it was difficult to distinguish the fetus in the amniotic fluid, he'd been moved to tears and filled with overwhelming joy.

He picked the pills up from the table, put them back in the pillbox, and cautiously lay back down. He heard the wild boar again, but this time was relieved because it sounded farther away. Lying precariously near the edge of the bed so as not to disturb his wife, he suddenly remembered that the owner of the house had mentioned a wild boar. Right after she gave him the piece of paper with the address on it, she said that some time ago a wild boar had come down from the back hills searching for something to eat.

"A wild boar?" His wife had repeated the owner's words as if she expected to actually see it rather than merely being alarmed by hearing about it.

"Yes, a wild boar. It is a common occurrence in a village in the hills," the owner added, "but even a boar has eyes to see and wouldn't attack a pretty young miss like you." His wife had blushed. Suppressing a smile and seeming happier, she looked up at the owner. Her husband also hid his feelings, but he was disgusted with the old crone's joke. His wife was obviously pregnant. Even a child could have seen that immediately.

Shortly after finding out about her pregnancy, he had been transferred to this branch of his company. It was actually quite desirable to be assigned to a branch, where it was easier to build one's career and rise in the company. The employees at the central office were well aware of this. This branch had a factory, and according to the openly declared policy of the company's president, a manager should be familiar with the production line.

"Isn't this a good offer? Won't you be more likely to be promoted two years from now?" the branch manager who had called him directly asked in his robust voice. This offer, with the relatively short dispatched period plus a good opportunity to be promoted, did indeed give him little reason to hesitate. Besides, this was during the ongoing economic depression when people were barely managing financially. He knew it would be wise to accept anything—anything that is, except resignation. Fortunately for him, his wife readily agreed.

"It would be a change. We'd live somewhere else for a little while. It shouldn't be so bad," she said, looking around the house where they'd lived since getting married. He felt a slight stirring in his heart. He felt that his work and his relationship with his wife had been following a repetitive operation manual. Familiar and comfortable, but it had become boring and uninteresting to the degree that insensitivity wasn't even an issue. He now read similar sentiments in his wife's face as she glanced absentmindedly around the house. They easily agreed to relocate. There were few decisions to make, and the process had progressed relatively smoothly.

Eventually, he got out of bed. He had been tossing and turning for some time, and was concerned that he'd wake his wife. His bare feet felt the freezing cold floor. Apparently the heat was turned off. The maintenance office controlled the heat in the most miserly way. It was often turned off, and even when it was running, it barely warmed the frigid air.

He walked toward the window, his cold feet braving the cold floor. Standing there, he saw the forest as black as coal, its paths, arbor, and scrub hidden in the darkness below. As soon as they'd moved into this house, he'd begun taking walks along a path that started in his backyard. A gentle hill formed a smooth slope that embraced the dense arbor. While out walking, he heard birds all around him. But in the dense forest it was hard to see them until they burst out of the trees and startled him.

However, it wasn't the sudden flight of birds or even the thought of a wild boar that caused him to stop walking in the forest. He wasn't afraid of a wild boar in whose existence he didn't really believe. It was the mayflies that hovered around him. He tried to brush them away by waving his hands, but he only smacked his own face. The harder he tried to hit them, the more he hit himself. Like a marionette, he shook his arms and legs wildly to no avail. The more ridiculously he struggled, the more insistently the winged insects multiplied and clung to him like a shadow.

The house they were living in had been recommended to him by the branch manager.

"Do you know what's most important for a renter. To get to know the owner of the house," he was told. The owner here was a professional landlady, but she was also the branch manager's mother. She had suggested this house that had been rented by a previously dispatched older alumnus. That man had worked at this branch for two years, been promoted, and returned to the central office. Hearing this, he signed the rental contract without even looking at the house. The owner, whom he and his wife met at the branch manager's office, handed him a slip of paper that was crumpled from having been folded and unfolded so often. On it was written the name of the street and the house number 111. She assured him that he'd be able to find it quite easily. "The block is so well organized that anyone can find houses there," she told him. "And you will discover the house is very quiet." His wife responded that she could imagine it must be fairly well soundproofed.

"At the moment there are no other renters," the owner said. His wife laughed, thinking this was a joke, and he, receiving the slip of paper, bowed from his waist to express his thanks.

"No, it's for us to thank you. We're grateful for having trustworthy people like you living there," the branch manager responded in a most pleasant manner.

It was a well-organized block, just as the owner had said. There was a row of houses on each side of the street. The houses on the right side had even numbers. The houses on the left had odd numbers. A female statue stood at the end of the road holding a torch, as though to signify the vanishing point. The first floor of the building block was mainly composed of stores whose entrances were narrowly canopied. None of them were open however, perhaps because it was a holiday. He proceeded to the left side of the road and checked the numbers, mumbling the number 111 as he searched for the house. The house at the beginning of the road was number 101, and the house at the end of the road, in the vicinity of the female statue holding a torch, was number 109. The houses on the other side of the road had only even numbers. He checked the numbers again. They definitely ended with the number 109. Completely clueless, he fingered the engraved number 109 on the acrylic panel.

As he walked up and down the road, he waved to his wife, who was sitting in the car waiting. She barely responded. In the next alley there was another section, but it was unthinkable that the owner would have given him a wrong address and number. He thought about phoning her, but decided it wouldn't be prudent to bother the elderly mother of the branch manager. Neither did he feel it would be wise to give the owner the impression that he had gotten lost in a place where everyone else had so easily managed to find their way. He strode up and down the road several times. Number 111 was nowhere to be found. He was confused.

Not many people lived in this neighborhood, but after looking for number 111 for a while, he finally saw someone. She was an older woman, slowly pushing a baby carriage along the road. Hesitantly, he approached her and asked where he might find number 111. The elderly woman's hearing seemed to be bad. She couldn't understand what he said. Frustrated, he abruptly shouted: "Number 111!" The woman shook her head and walked away. Watching as she waddled off with the carriage, he couldn't help but laugh. In fact he almost cried, but this wasn't a matter for either laughter or tears. He heard a dog barking somewhere in the building, and this gave him hope. It was a sure sign that someone was living there, although the place looked totally desolate.

The branch manager wasn't in his office. No one who would know his whereabouts was around either. He was perplexed. He saw that darkness was hovering over the canopies and felt that the canopies were only momentarily preventing the darkness from fully descending. After a long time the branch manager returned his call, and having talked with his mother on the phone, explained that number 111 couldn't be seen from the road but was accessible only through number 109.

"You weren't told that?" the branch manager asked.

"I have a poor sense of direction," he responded, as he if needed to make an excuse for himself.

The key to number 109 was under the flowerpot by the front door. He imagined earthworms squirming in the damp earth under the pot. He retrieved the key and wiped his muddied hand on the name plate.

As he opened the door, he was pounced on by a gigantic affectionate animal. He groaned and stepped back, as the dog licked his face with its long tongue. He forcefully removed the creature that was practically hugging him. Since his wife had just confirmed her pregnancy, this was a time when they had to be extremely cautious. Attempting to ease her mind, he forced himself to laugh while his heart pounded. The dog began to lick his neck. He saw that the dog was wagging its tail and decided it would not bite him, but this display of affection could nevertheless be somewhat intimidating. So he held the giant dog tightly as he called his wife in. She started to enter, then abruptly stopped in surprise.

"Don't be frightened. This is really a very gentle dog," he told her as he opened his arms wide and enthusiastically hugged the dog in an effort meant to both reassure his wife and restrain this overly affectionate canine that was bigger than him.

"It's not a dog, it's a monster!" his wife cried. The dog showed its teeth and growled at her.

"No, it's a dog. Really, a very gentle one indeed. You know, I think a dog like this could very well be a gatekeeper in heaven, and we'd need to pass by him to enter. So passing by this dog now, we are about to enter heaven."

Ordinarily, he didn't at all care for overly sentimental expressions like, "my heavenly home" or "my angelic baby," but at this moment when he so desperately needed to comfort his wife, these expressions slipped smoothly and easily out of his mouth.

"Please just this once," he implored. "Believe me, after this, we'll be in heaven."

She bit her lip as though determined to enter this heaven and blocked her ears so as not to hear the dog barking as it vigorously wagged its tail. This big, noisy dog was indeed gentle, and he actually felt warm while hugging it. He gently patted its head and continued on down to the basement. There he found a door that opened into the backyard and discovered a trail leading to the forest. At the beginning of the trail there appeared a small, three-story building attached like an appendage to the wall of number 109. Number 111.

The house wasn't much of a heaven, but it did undeniably have some of the attributes of heaven. The forest in back of it was filled with tall trees and looked like part of a man-made garden, but it also felt rather somber. One side of the house was attached to a wall so that no light could enter, but the whole other side consisted of windows that provided an incredible view of the forest. The kitchen cabinet held neatly arranged old dishes. An old-fashioned bedspread covered the bed. The old chairs looked rather charming, although they turned out to be squeaky and uncomfortable. Forgetting her exhaustion, his wife scrutinized each of the dishes in the cupboard.

"I wanted to buy teacups like these," she said, holding up a cup with a blue floral design. "We will drink from these teacups every day."

It had been a long time since he'd felt relaxed. He and his wife looked at each other and laughed. But the dog interrupted their laughter. It stayed at the front door barking. The wooden door handle began to move. His wife stared at it, and he immediately called the owner.

"Oh, that dog is so friendly. If you stroke his head and hug him, he immediately falls in love with you and follows you everywhere. Anyway, it would never bite you. Please tell your young lady not to worry."

"My wife is pregnant. Could you possibly put the dog on a leash?" He emphasized the word *pregnant* and would have spoken more forcefully if he hadn't remembered that the owner was also the branch manager's mother.

"On a leash," the owner repeated in a displeased voice. "That dog guards number 109 and number 111. Both places are under my care. We've never had a robbery in either of them thanks to that dog. It's really a gentle creature. It's never bitten so much as a man's shadow. The real problem is that he is *too* friendly."

His wife looked at him accusingly as he hung up the phone. "Now I've lost my freedom to go outside because of that dog," she complained. This embarrassed him. He kicked the front door in anger, and the dog, which had been waiting and groaning on the other side of it, finally stole away. But the groaning sound lingered so vividly in his ears that it disturbed his sleep that night, and from then on he began to suffer from insomnia. He slept for only three or four hours each night, and most nights, the dog came to the front door and barked.

He heard the cry of the wild boar again. This time the sound was neither farther away nor closer than before. Instead of wandering about the neighborhood looking for food, the animal seemed to be announcing its presence by prowling around the same spot again and again. Except for that one cry, it was suspiciously quiet outside. There were no passing cars or barking dogs. Perhaps the police had rushed in and shot the boar with a tranquilizer gun or captured it with a net. But there had been no siren. In the palpable silence, he imagined someone being attacked by the wild boar on the empty road. Frightening as this was, he knew he himself wasn't in danger because he lived on the third floor, unlike his neighbors who lived on lower floors..

But as he was returning to the bedroom, he heard a scratching on the wooden front door. Slowly he approached it. The sound was more like a body slamming against the door than a scratching. He could hear an animal's soft breathing, its frightened groans. He peered through the fisheye lens, and saw the dog roaming around out there. It too must have heard the wild boar and come running up the stairway. Unnerved by the dog's whimpering, he bolted the front door, slid the latch closed, and locked the windows. He kicked the front door, trying to get rid of the dog. A mistake. The dog let out a low growl. In the dark the painted white wooden door shone like a shield, and he was using it as a shield as he confronted the dog in the darkness. He'd led such an uninteresting life, and now he felt he was making himself ridiculous by taking on none other than a dog as his ultimate adversary.

In his office the next day, writing documents, he remembered the sound of the wild boar the night before. Was there anyone else in the neighborhood who'd heard the wild snarling and snorting? Someone must have looked out a window and seen the boar running down the road.

"Did you hear a sound last night?" he asked the junior colleague, who sat next to him and was the tenant in number 109.

"Indescribable."

He was pleased to hear his junior colleague's response and turned toward him. No one else had mentioned the wild boar. Even his sensitive wife had slept soundly while the boar was wailing. He'd almost begun to think that he had heard it in a dream. Were he and the dog the only ones who'd been frightened by the sound?

"I barely managed to get up this morning after drinking so much," his junior colleague told him. "Even now I feel nauseous. I must still smell bad, too, huh?"

Only then did he remember that there had been a dinner party the previous night. The branch manager had made a spontaneous suggestion that everyone should stop at a bar on their way home, but he couldn't join them because of his wife. She was too afraid of the dog to venture outside during the day, and she frequently called him at work to ask when he'd be returning home. If he arrived later than the promised time, she'd greet him with her eyes swollen from crying. She complained that living in this place was like being in prison, and she urged him to move back to the city.

Now he began to realize that most of the office workers were talking about the party last night. They were joking and laughing about everything they'd shared. Even though he hadn't participated, he appreciated their conversations about the branch manager's pitiful singing skills, the way he danced with his fists punching the air, and his boldly hugging the female office workers. However, there were other comments that confused him. He couldn't determine whether they were about things that had really happened or were merely jokes.

He simply smiled at everything they said and slowly finished the documents he was working on. His eyes burned, making it difficult for him to see, and he concluded that this was probably due to his insomnia. He applied eye drops, which ran down his cheeks like tears. He was drying them with a tissue when his wife called. She was weeping.

"The dog barked all morning in front of the front door, and I am having contractions every hour." He imagined the frightened dog scratching at the wooden door.

"Has the wild boar come again?" he asked urgently.

"Wild boar? A wild boar is coming too?" his wife screamed and began to cry bitterly and so loudly that she could be heard by the others. He glanced around the office, embarrassed. His junior colleague caught his eye and cocked his head.

"I am too frightened living here," his wife sobbed. "If I feel this much fear, can you imagine how our baby will feel? It's all because of that dog. Now I won't even be able to get out to take a taxi when the contractions start coming closer together. I might have to deliver the baby all alone in this small house. It's driving me crazy thinking about it."

"What do you mean alone? The landlady lives nearby," he said, but this did nothing to console her. Neither, for that matter, was he convinced that the landlady was someone who could be depended upon.

"How could I ever trust someone like this landlady who turns off the heat in the middle of night and allows a monstrous animal to roam around freely scaring her tenants to death?" his wife irritably replied. He forced a smile, and told her that he'd be on his way home soon. He asked her to be patient and wait for him just a little longer. Then he hung up.

He had to submit a form for early leave to the branch manager who looked at him and frowned.

"Do you know how many times you have made this kind of a request?"

"My wife is having contractions."

"I have three children. With the first one, I was there with my wife all through her contractions. For the second one, I was there right before the delivery. The third one, I couldn't be there at all due to business. The contractions won't bring the baby any quicker. With you or without you the baby will arrive on time, and it's not going to happen right away. You're taking this too seriously." The first time that he'd had to leave early because of his wife, the branch manager had simply laughed warmly and told him it wasn't easy becoming a father.

"I heard that you were one of the most diligent workers at the central office. You also have a good work record. That's why I chose you." He nodded his head, agreeing that he was diligent, and the branch manager glared at him. This manager had been born and grew up in this region. He was determined, stubborn and had a strong commitment to the community. "You like it here, right? You'd like to live here for a long time, right?"

"It's because of the dog. My wife has become so sensitive because of the dog," he replied, somewhat perplexed. The branch manager looked at him as though he was being absolutely ridiculous, and he realized that there was no sense in his trying to explain any further. He knew that this wasn't the best time to talk about it. He left the annoyed manager and returned to his desk.

"Do you like dogs?" he asked his junior colleague while putting his unfinished documents in his bag.

"I like humans better than dogs."

"Me too."

"Be patient. Someday it will die," the junior colleague said, laughing.

"Will it?" he asked as he closed his bag. "Will it one day just die all on its own?"

"The manager is crazy about that dog," his junior colleague said, lowering his voice. "By the way, you should take some sleeping pills. You look terrible."

He nodded. How fervently he wished for a nice, long, deep sleep.

He'd never raised a dog and had almost no knowledge of them. But he did know that dogs had gone into outer space before humans. He knew that dogs had delivered explosives during the war, and that they frightened soldiers. During the war, soldiers who tried to escape from prison camps were caught more quickly by dogs than by the guards. Perhaps most significant of all, he knew that in medieval times, dogs were buried with their owners to guide them on their way to heaven.

When he opened the door to number 109, the dog rushed to him to be hugged, wagging its tail. It had been a long time since he'd had such a friendly hug. He gently patted the dog's head. The dog began to sniff loudly. It was definitely interested in the smell emanating from the black bag in his hand. He passed through 109 and came to the outside of number 111. The dog obediently followed him. It was true, as the owner had said, that the problem with this dog was that it was too affectionate with humans.

As he approached the entrance to the trail he met a group of villagers with water bottles sitting at the base of a tree trunk.

"Which way to the spring water?" he asked the villagers.

"That way," one man from the group said pointing off to the right. "It's really close." He bowed slightly to thank him.

"You have such a big dog."

"Yes, he is big and very gentle," he said proudly, and the dog wagged its tail.

"You should feel safe enough with him."

He smiled. He didn't reply.

The dog stayed close to him at first. Then, as it got used to his pace, it went ahead of him and stopped, waiting and wagging its tail. When it wanted to mark its territory, the dog went far enough ahead that he didn't have to stop and wait for it to urinate. Every so often the dog hurried on ahead but never urged him to walk faster. Nor did the dog pester him to take a different path. It simply rambled along a few steps ahead of him. He felt so in tune with this dog. It was as if they'd been strolling along together for years.

He met no one else on his way to the spring, and when he arrived there, he took a path off to the side overgrown with tangled weeds and tall trees. It was a rough, wild place rampant with weeds and branches. Poked and scratched by the branches, the dog winced and looked up at him. He patted it gently on the head to reassure it. The sky between the trees was getting dark. It was time to stop.

"Anyone there?" he shouted into empty space. A moment later, his voice echoed back to him. Gently, he patted the dog again and found a stretch of flat ground where he could sit. The dog circled him. He took a chunk of meat from the plastic bag. The dog came closer and sniffed. He thought it might be an unfamiliar smell for the dog, that the dog might refuse to eat it. He hoped it would refuse to eat it. He hadn't come this way for a long time, and this time it had felt more peaceful than ever before. The dog licked the meat several times with its long tongue and began to eat. He felt sad, but made no attempt to stop it. While it chowed down with great enthusiasm, he tied one end of a rope around its neck and the other end around the thick trunk of a tree. Having eaten the whole chunk of meat, the dog opened its mouth and begged for more. It roamed around the spot for a long time, and every so often breathed heavily with its tongue lolling. Then it began to bark. He turned to look at the place that the dog had barked at. He didn't want to be disturbed by an intruder, but only darkness was approaching. Then fear began to take hold of him. He'd once heard that a dog could recognize the messenger of death coming to get its owner.

After he'd been sitting on the grass for some time, his pants felt wet and his back was freezing. But somehow both the cold and the dampness felt bearable, as if he'd been cold and damp for most of his life. The dog continued barking, and every time the sound of distant barking echoed back. Hearing the echo, the dog whined and struggled to free itself from the rope again and again, until it was overcome by exhaustion. It grew quiet. He watched as the dog fell exhausted on the grass, vomiting up what it had eaten, foaming at the mouth, defecating, urinating, shivering, moaning. He watched as it gasped and panted, its long tongue craving water. He hugged its soft, warm, trembling body. Lying in his arms, the dog gave a sudden fierce groan. Surprised and shocked, he laid it down on the ground and rose to leave. The dog let out one low last wail, as though calling to him as he hurried away down the slope.

The trees stood dense and motionless, their dark blue branches hanging downward. But when the wind started to blow, the trees shuddered as if threatening to fall. Nervous birds exploded from the trees and the sounds of insects grew louder. Then the sound of a groaning dog reached his ears. He looked back in the direction of the sound but saw only the dark, shadowy movements of trees and leaves.

The farther he walked, the denser the pine forest became. He continued on for some time, until the forest turned into something completely different. Sharp tree branches began to strike him. Bushes and trees of every size surrounded him. He wondered if he was going around in circles, returning again and again to the same place. It was like a sense of déjà vu. The deeper the forest became, the more the trails looked the same. Everywhere he saw tall trees that blocked out the sky, he heard the ominous cries of birds, and felt high, hard weeds sticking him through his long pants. The trails were barely connected, then suddenly disconnected, then reconnected by the trodden-down grass.

"Anyone out there?" he shouted. Moments later, his voice returned to him in several layers and more birds flew out and scattered. He was exhausted. The forest held him in a tight grip. He couldn't move a step farther. He had to admit that he was lost in a completely unfamiliar world.

The forest absorbed the darkness and disclosed it to the earth. In the pitch black he could just barely make out two separate trails. One long, curved route led toward the pine forest. The other trail, tangled with thorny vines, curved and sloped downward. Given these choices, he should have searched not for the right path, but the fastest one. He bent low in order to pass through the bush-infested forest. He tried to protect his head with his arms, but was nevertheless attacked by the hard, spiky branches that prodded and poked his body. He bent lower. He tried to be careful not to step on the slippery grass, but he fell several times, landing on his hip.

As he groped his way through the forest, he saw a huge, dark shadow hanging, lingering in space in front of him. It looked like a dark cloud, and seeing that it remained low, he assumed that a rain shower was imminent. But as he continued on his way, the cloud, which had been blocking his sight, followed him. It grew larger. It approached him, and then suddenly scattered in all directions. The mayflies collided with his face. He waved his arms to brush them away, but they adhered to his hair and his clothes. The more vigorously he tried to brush them away, the greater the number that attacked him. He took off his suit jacket, and holding it in both hands, waved it like a fan. For an instant, it looked as if they were going to disperse, but then they landed again on his skin. The incessant buzzing in his ears was even worse than their assault on his face. It felt as if they were building a nest in his ears. He scratched with his fingernails, but it did nothing to alleviate the itching.

He started running, trying to escape from the flies, but running only resulted in his being snared by the low tangle of branches. His foot was caught, and again he fell, scraping his already sore knees. He stepped on a patch of slippery grass, slid, and fell again. His sides throbbed with pain, and still the may-flies continued their attack. He didn't realize until he was out of breath that he couldn't escape from them no matter how fast he ran because they weren't merely chasing him. They were swarm-ing all over him. They were nesting in him. There was no way that he could escape them or defeat their solid community. He leaned against a dead tree and gasped. The flies flew into his open mouth, his nostrils. He was inhaling them. It was disgusting, and there seemed to be no end to it. When he managed to catch his breath, he coughed up thick phlegm.

He was now thoroughly disenchanted with the forest. It con-tained something other than the sounds of wind, birds, insects, and distant streams. There was also a murmuring, a nearby whis-pering human voice or a distant, sorrowful cry. Someone seemed to be coming down the trail toward him. He shouted, asking if anybody was out there, but only his own voice answered.

Cautiously listening to these sounds of the forest, it came to him how much he missed the sounds of the forest of skyscrap-ers, the noise of running cars and air conditioners in the heart of the city. The deeper he wandered into the forest, the better he began to understand the city. He decided that the noises of the city were more honest. They hid nothing. The city was in some ways a good analogy for the forest. Even on a fine day the city sky would never clear up. Endless traffic filled the air with exhaust fumes. The trees that lined the streets were always covered with dust. All this well-articulated scenery was familiar to him. It felt so much more intimate than natural scenery.

Because he wasn't conscious of its artificiality, it seemed as natural to him as the natural world. The air pollution, the iden-tical trees lining the streets at regular intervals, the slices of sky visible between the skyscrapers—this is what he'd experienced growing up in the city. Blue skies, clean air, vast open fields, and the leaves of trees trembling in the wind were alien to him. Until now he'd always been surrounded by hard asphalt, black sewer water, back alleys at night redolent with the smell of left-over food, the rushing taxis with headlights glaring, belching out pollution. He realized how much he disliked the little suburbs with their heavy silence, their cold air, and their tree-dense forests. Compared to this dark, reticent forest in which everything was concealed, the city was practically celestial, with its brightly lit streets.

His wife would never imagine that he was out wandering in the forest. She'd be concerned about the dog, fearful it would show up at any moment. She'd be trying to remain patient as she endured the intensifying pain of her contractions. But he too was in pain. She might have been continually calling him, not being able to find anyone else to help her. He regretted that he hadn't brought his mobile phone with him, but he hadn't wanted to tell his wife about his walk with the dog, and he'd had no idea it would take this long. Slowly, he looked around at the trees swaying in the wind. The forest, now fully robed in darkness, stared back at him expressionlessly.

He began to move his feet. He had to keep going. Only then would he find his way out. He followed the slope. This, he thought, would lead him toward the lower side of the forest or the route leading deep into the valley. He was walking frantically when he heard a strange noise. It was a sniffing, a *kung kung* sound punctuated by unpleasant gasps, the sound of a large body breaking through tree branches. There was a wild boar in the forest. There was also a large, dying dog. He dropped to his knees in fear. It was impossible to determine which direction the sound was coming from. It seemed to be coming from all different directions. He was sure that either the hungry wild boar or the dog returning from the dead was drawing near.

Suddenly he felt he was going to sneeze. He bent over trying to stop it and tasted pine sap as needles pricked his face. He pressed his chest to prevent the sneeze and continued walking downhill through the dense forest trees and bushes that blocked his sight. He couldn't stop walking. He couldn't control his fear. He hoped if he continued this way he'd eventually come to a village. Meanwhile, the strange sound had ceased, and because it had ceased, he wondered if it had ever existed to begin with. It might have been his fear that caused him to assume that every forest sound was an animal's cry.

On his way down the slope, his foot caught on something. Something that was both hard and soft, both white and shiny under the moonlight. It looked like a large rock or perhaps an uncovered grave. But it was the dog, the dog tied by a rope lying there with its legs stretched out and stiffened. He dropped to the ground and trembled uncontrollably. He smoked a cigarette to overcome the sudden cold he felt. Fumbling in his pocket, he dropped his house key. It hit the ground and slid out of sight. To search for it, he had to clumsily grope through the rough, dark bushes and weeds. Finally, he gave up and drew deeply on his cigarette. He exhaled, and the smoke scattered by the wind attracted the mayflies. Once more they gathered around him. He held up his lighter flame to kill them, but they weren't deterred. They swarmed endlessly.

He touched a pine branch with the flame. It didn't catch fire easily, but after some time it began to generate white smoke. Soon it began to crackle and burn. He tossed the burning branch deep into the forest. It took a while for the fire to spread. He felt less cold and uncontrollably sleepy, which was strange. It had been so long since he'd been able to get a good night's sleep, or had even felt like sleeping at all. With half-closed eyes, he gazed at the forest that surrounded him. The thick darkness reached out and covered him like a warm blanket. Finally, after so long a time, he could sleep soundly again.

JUNGLE GYM

THE AIRPORT WAS crowded. People standing in front of the gate called out the names on the signs they were holding up, signs of all different sizes and bearing a variety of names. One of these signs caught his attention, not because his own name was on it but because of the ridiculous spelling, which any speaker of his native tongue would have found humorous. The initial and final consonants were transposed, as were the right and left strokes of the vowels. A man, who appeared to be Chinese, was holding the sign and looking as sullen as a child being punished.

He laughed quietly. The off-the-wall spelling of the sign was for him an amusing welcome, a welcome that made him feel less exhausted and nervous after his long flight and his arrival in this unfamiliar city. But it also made him aware that he'd just arrived in a city where his native tongue was ludicrously imitated and misspelled. Also, having arrived on a thirteen-hour flight, the local time indicated only four hours had passed since his departure the previous afternoon. He was exhausted from jet lag, and for whatever reason, he sensed that his condition wouldn't improve during his stay in this city. A group of sign holders left accompanied by their guests, and a new group filed into its place, but the Chinese-seeming sign holder remained.

He was still looking for a sign with his name on it when it suddenly occurred to him that the misspelled name might be Director Baik's. He adjusted the positions of the letters and lines, discovered it was Baik's name, and thought that this sign might be meant for him. Hesitantly, he approached the sign holder and pointed at the name.

"This is I," he stated rather unconvincingly. Except for being able to say, "thank you," in order to be polite,.he barely knew the language spoken in this city. He was even awkward with the common foreign language that most of the people knew. The man stared at him, then turned and led him to a black van in the airport parking lot before returning to the terminal with another sign. Since he hadn't been given any explanation, he surmised that there was someone else to be picked up. He sat there waiting without giving it any further thought. Though it was still early evening, it was completely dark, and so chilly in the car that he was shivering even with the heat turned on.

The lodging to which he was to be taken had been recommended by Director Baik.

"Do you like traveling?" Baik had asked, starting off the conversation, as usual, by asking an uncomfortable question. Since in these situations he couldn't tell what Baik was up to, he decided that, rather than replying immediately, it would be better to wait for what followed.

"Is there anything better for relaxing your mind than traveling?" Baik continued as he handed him the airplane tickets. "I would appreciate it if you'd make time in your busy schedule for a business trip."

Baik then chuckled loudly as though he'd just made a joke. He laughed too. In fact Baik's asking him for a favor was more or less a joke. "The only thing you have to do is sign the order form for the business trip," he was told. He looked at the order form under the airplane tickets. Everything had been filled in except his signature and the date of his return.

"I envy you. I myself have always wished to take off just as you can now." The truth of the matter was that he envied Baik, who could order him to do this.

"The reason for your taking this trip, at this particular time," Baik added, "is that we need to amend the accounting system. It's inevitable, isn't it? It's not at all easy to calibrate the busy schedules of the two people involved in two different cities. You know?" Baik said this as if he was reflecting upon the issue himself, trying to understand it rather than explaining it to someone else. In any case, he knew Baik was ordering him to make this business trip, and he nodded in agreement.

"So what does it mean when the person involved is on a business trip?" Baek asked looking directly at him.

"It means he's not available to be issued a summons."

There were widespread rumors that an inspection was about to take place at any moment. Every time the office door opened, it was feared that the inspectors had arrived. His only responsibility was to secure the double bookkeeping and to write neatly when recording the logistics.

"The inspectors have many questions," Baik went on. "That is their job. They have to scrutinize your work by examining your papers and your bookkeeping. They ask questions, and they listen as, typically, you reply that you do not remember. But that won't work this time." Baik said.

He looked at Baik curiously as though to ask why, and Baik continued:

"You'll be on a trip, right? There will be no one to answer them about the matter. You'll be gone, and the others know only what they're responsible for." He too knew only what he'd been doing, which was dealing with the papers, receipts, and contracts that Baik handed him and doing the low level daily, weekly and monthly accounting. Again, he nodded agreeably.

"How long should I be on this business trip?"

"Regrettably, it won't be too long. The internal inspection, as you know, is often just a formality." Then, feigning sincerity, Baik added: "When the inspection finishes, you will certainly return to me."

"Certainly I will," he responded immediately. He sincerely hoped more than anything to be ordered to return as soon as possible. When he hurriedly started packing up his things, the senior colleague who sat next to him asked in a low voice, "Is this Mr. Baik's order?"

He nodded. He had only a few things to pack, as he had no real job to do at his destination.

"Do not rely on Baik too much," the senior colleague whispered.

He nodded again. He didn't really trust Baik, but he didn't distrust him either. He simply preferred to rely on him. But this trip had nothing to do with relying or not relying on Baik. He simply had no choice.

"But why do you speak so negatively about Mr. Baik?" he asked as he packed his stationery. His colleague stared at him as if he were naive.

"Mr. Baik will use any means to protect his own interests," the senior colleague said, lowering his voice as though he was passing on classified information.

He didn't completely agree with his colleague, because it wasn't only Mr. Baik. He knew there were also others in the company who would make sure they'd never suffer any loss. Since joining this company, he had been working on the sales statements, contracts and receipts, and he knew that the accounting system protected all of them. He generally followed Baik's orders, most of which involved the bookkeeping methods. He was ordered to use methods with which he was acquainted but had never used before.

"There are no legal issues here?" he had asked, not being aware in the beginning that questioning Baik's orders wouldn't be appreciated. Later, he came to realize that Baik regarded that question as an expression of agreement. He only wished that the methods weren't illegal, or that if they were illegal, they'd at least be handled clandestinely and not so openly disclosed as to put him in the position of having to acknowledge them.

"Legal issues?" Baik repeated. "Do you know who directs our work—in other words, who our employer is?"

He pointed at the company structure map on the office wall and asked, "Shouldn't it be the person at the top of the map?"

Baik laughed. "So, then, who is that person?"

"Pardon?"

Baik stopped laughing and said: "This isn't a quiz. I myself don't know the answer. Sometimes there are too many, and other times there are none. But this is important."

He didn't understand why the number changed so Baik explained.

"The fact is that we don't know who our employer is. That's what I mean. Now, do you think that's all, or is there something else that we don't know?"

"Pardon?"

"I really don't know what I'm doing. And you, do you know? What I do know is that I chose this job for a living. That's all."

"Then what should I do for you?" he asked, still not fully understanding what Baik had been saying to him about their employer's absence from the map. Yet, as he listened to Baik's explanation, he began to feel some weird sense of camaraderie with this man who'd previously been so distant from him.

"What would you say if I offered to guarantee you a successful career?" Baik asked.

"I'd ask how you could guarantee it since you're not the employer. Then, I'd ask you about the conditions and the benefits and what my responsibilities would be."

Baik laughed heartily at this and said: "Exactly. That is all you would have wanted me to tell you. Now the only thing remaining is for you to learn this method from me." Then Baik handed him a thick account book.

His wife seemed delighted to hear about his business trip.

"Everybody wants to visit that city. The rest of us only dream about going there, but you are lucky enough to be given the opportunity. You will also naturally make foreign friends while living and working there," she said.

"Do you want me to have foreign friends?" he asked. She hadn't meant to say what she did, and she merely responded to his question by laughing a little. Momentarily, he did think about taking her with him. This was a business trip in name only as he didn't have an assigned task and was only to spend time there as if he were on holiday. If Baik had told him the truth, there was only one purpose for his going away. He really wasn't thinking about making foreign friends while there alone.

During their nearly ten years of marriage, he and his wife had made few trips together. Twice they went on brief excursions organized by tour agencies with schedules that required them to rise early in the morning, ride on huge buses, and get off at historical sites and famous places. After brief visits, they were rushed back to the buses that then carried them to a mushroom factory, a latex factory, a jewelry store, or shopping centers, where they listened to sales talks disguised as lectures and were allowed to roam around in shopping centers. These were cheap package tours. They especially remembered their uncomfortable experience of riding on smelly elephants, which they did only because it was included in the package deal. This ordeal was duly recorded in a photo of them staring straight ahead and smiling, despite the fact that they were feeling ill from the terrible odors and were frightened by the ground vibrating beneath them. After that, the thought of traveling always reminded them of the odor of elephant feces, the discomfort of the vibrating earth, the sound of jingling beads, and the varied colors of the elephants' hats.

Thus they soon despaired of organized package tours offered by travel agencies and decided to go on a trip by themselves. This started out smoothly in the beginning, but as time went by, their moods became heavier and heavier until they doubled the weight of their backpacks. He became so angry with his wife that he refused to talk to her. After a while he did make his peace with her, not because he felt sorry for her, but rather from the unbearable discomfort of the silence. But soon they began arguing again over trivial matters and stopped talking to each other again.

Traveling made him realize that even his countenance and his tone of voice reflected his job. His fastidiousness, stinginess, nervousness, and lassitude all resulted from his having worked for so long as an accountant. When he felt tired and argued with his wife, these characteristics rose to the surface. The serious thinking that he did in his spare time, along with the scars he suffered from his wife's anger during that trip, disillusioned him. He decided that inviting his wife on this trip wasn't a good idea.

According to Baik, the internal inspection was only a formality. The inspectors would, as usual, prolong their time there in order to frighten the persons directly involved before merely cautioning or warning them in order to demonstrate their goodwill. The process would end with no real result. When he returned from this so-called business trip, he'd have no free time at all. Inspections were infrequent, so he was thankful for this unexpected chance to travel now, while he was still young, and with his expenses paid by the company. He also thought of this as an opportunity to spend money. He'd never wasted anything. In his accounting job, he'd learned that time and money were to be systematically controlled, efficiently used, saved, and never consumed or wasted. He decided not to waste this unique opportunity by riding an elephant or enduring trivial emotional confrontations with his wife.

He told her that she could visit him if he had to prolong his trip, but he felt sure this wouldn't happen. He also told her that they could then visit not only the city where he was staying but other cities in the vicinity as well. His wife looked at him and laughed again. Her laughter gave him no indication that she was criticizing him for his unlikely suggestions. Nor did it express any expectation or even sadness. They had merely been fantasizing about taking advantage of another chance to make a trip together. She laughed just to show that she understood what he was really saying. This made him realize that he too expected little from this hastily arranged trip, despite the exaggerated joy and pleasure he was expressing.

After a long time the Chinese-looking man returned to the car with a foreign couple. While their escort started the car and then waited for the traffic light to change, the foreign couple smiled and greeted him. Timidly, he responded with the few words that a non-native speaker would be expected to know. Every so often the couple, who were seated facing him, intentionally looked at him, inviting him to join in their conversation. He tried to be polite by smiling in return, but then turned his head toward the darkness outside and refused to talk to them. It was completely dark outside now, and he could see only the reflection of his own tense face in the window. He was agonizing about having to ride in this small van with this foreign couple all the way to their shared lodgings, where he'd be staying with them for days, and seeing them often in the dining room or corridor or washroom. The van pulled in and stopped at the end of a dark alley where he could barely manage to see a row of similarly shaped houses. Exotic writing embossed on a bronze panel beside the entrance was clearly legible even in the dark. He studied it closely and with some difficulty. He was concerned that he wouldn't be able to find the house again unless he memorized the address.

"Mr. Baik has asked after you."

Surprised to hear this, he turned to look behind him. It was the Chinese looking escort who had said this, but he suddenly didn't look Chinese anymore. Despite his faulty pronunciation, the man was obviously speaking his native tongue. He remembered the misspelling on the sign and once again decided that the man might indeed be Chinese. It didn't really matter to him, however, so he gave up thinking about it. Baik had merely told him that the place where he was going to stay was run by someone with whom he had a slight connection. Still, he felt it strange that Baik had sent this message through this man with whom he had only a slight connection, instead of calling him directly on his phone. At first, he conjectured it might be the situation with the inspectors that made it difficult for Baik to contact him directly. This made him uncomfortable, but then he remembered his own timidity and inability to disagree or complain, and decided it was quite understandable that Baik had called this man instead of him. But now he became aware of the Chinese-looking man observing him like a security guard watching a suspicious person. He immediately moved on to the entrance of the lodgings.

That night he couldn't fall asleep, but couldn't decide whether it was because of the long journey, the anxiety of being in a foreign place, or simply the time difference. It was just past midnight. In his own city, he'd have been on the train to work at this hour, as he had been for the past fifteen years. He hardly slept through the night. The old heating system in the house groaned constantly. There was a heavy squeaking noise in the corridor, the cry of the exhausted radiator pipes, and an undistinguishable scratching sound coming from the walls and ceiling. Along with making loud noises, the heating system wasn't functioning properly, and the blankets provided enough warmth for only the spring and autumn months. He was shivering, he was congested, he had a sore throat. This wasn't at all the picture that Baik had painted. This was a place fit only for long-term travelers on very low budgets.

Half awake and half dreaming, he heard someone knocking at the door. It was the Chinese-looking escort who had brought him to these lodgings. Although he hadn't requested a wakeup call, he didn't complain. He didn't want to waste the day sleeping. The man offered him some hard bread and a drink and told him about several places that Baik often visited. He allowed the man to say whatever it was he had to say and saw no reason to respond, nor did the man seem to expect him to be sociable. Besides, he found it almost impossible to understand the man's poor pronunciation and his confusing combination of their two languages. He did, however, manage to decipher that Baik had stayed there for several months. This aroused his curiosity. When could it have been that Baik had had that much time to spend there? He didn't inquire further about this, though, if only because he didn't want to continue in conversation with this character.

After breakfast, he hurried out to the street as if on his usual way to work. He worried as he walked nonchalantly along, dropping into stores with shoddy goods aimed so directly at travelers' wallets. He decided to look at the stores, restaurants, and places Baik had recommended. But he also thought he'd prefer to visit the famous places of the region first, since he was on call to return home at any time, including perhaps even that very day. Some time ago, he'd read a foreign guidebook that compared this city with his hometown. Now, in only one day, he discovered the similarities. He saw the tired faces of hardworking laborers and the many angry faces. He heard loud, aggressive voices. He noted warm, spontaneous characteristics, especially among the shopkeepers. However, he didn't agree that these similarities existed only between this city and his hometown. He was convinced that in all cities, the only people who leisurely strolled in the streets with contented expressions were either the tourists or the elderly, who had nothing else to do.

He walked as unhurriedly as a tourist along a four-lane street lined on both sides with ground-floor stores in low buildings. He turned into a back alley, and there discovered the original buildings from the past, and even some historical remains from ancient times. Breathtaking beauty emanated from this decay. It was as if the ruins had been deliberately left standing, instead of being repossessed by the city, and this effort to preserve the decaying past prevented it from moving into the future.

This entire exotic environment calmed rather than excited him. He visited all the places Baik had visited, ate where Baik had eaten, and purchased items in stores where Baik had shopped. He strode about the city until he was exhausted, took breaks at cafes and studied a map to find his way back to his lodgings. He constantly consulted the map, as if finding his lodgings without getting lost was his one and only goal. He didn't speak the local language, and people hardly understood when he did attempt to speak a word or two. Perhaps this was the reason he had the same kind of headache upon returning to his lodgings he usually

experienced after finishing his day's work of bookkeeping and
dealing with contracts full of complicated numbers.

As time went on, he became acclimated to the mysteriously
foreign street scenes. He began to think of himself as a first-time
visitor from a distant land, adapting fairly well to the local food
and finding his way around. He felt proud of himself, but also
realized he was too old for such childish pretending. Moreover,
it was Baik, not he, who had ordered this trip. He'd only had
to accept the airplane tickets, the schedule and guidebook with
which Baik had presented him, and proceed to wander around
the city to his heart's content. Realizing this brought back vivid
memories of the elephant ride. Once more he smelled the elephant feces, heard the cheap beads jangling on the elephants'
hats, and felt the earth vibrating beneath him.

Returning to his lodgings, he wrote up a brief report about
the places he'd visited, the food he'd eaten, and the insignificant
items he'd purchased. He attached his meticulously organized
receipts. It wasn't necessary to write a report, but he was determined to keep a record to show that he had followed Baik's
orders. Then he phoned his wife to report to her.

"That's good. You must be having fun," his wife replied after
listening to him. She wasn't being sarcastic. Her tone of voice
made him think that, yes, he was dutifully following his schedule
and obediently carrying out orders to visit tourist attractions,
but no, he wasn't enjoying himself. He was in fact suppressing a
strong desire to return home.

As he hung up, he felt that he'd been forced to come to this
strange place and that by naively falling into temptation, he'd
participated in the conspiracy. He was reminded that his life
had always been determined by other people. He became angry,
not only because others had controlled his life, but also because

he knew how secure he felt when he was indeed controlled by someone else.

He thought that perhaps the problem at his office had become worse after he left. While he was wandering about in this unfamiliar city, he also feared that the responsibility for the accounting problem might fall entirely upon him. He realized that imagining the possibility of such a conspiracy might be just a fantasy because he wasn't there to help solve the problem, and he fervently hoped that it was just a fantasy. He also considered the measures that might be taken to solve the problem and wondered whether Baik would correct the error himself, or order someone else to take care of it, or possibly just leave it unresolved. As for the bookkeeping, it was obvious that Baik would have to order someone to take over and correct the errors in his absence. All of this reminded him of when he first started working with Baik.

Now none of his thoughts were clear, and he was becoming more and more confused. He regretted leaving as he had, without preparing a way to defend himself in case he was accused. At the same time he hated himself for being so stingy and rigid about spending from the beginning of this trip, despite his initial intention to spend money and enjoy himself. He blamed his headache on the cold and the previous night's accumulated fatigue. He lay down with his clothes on. He had a runny nose, a ringing in the ears and a toothache, but he decided he was simply catching a cold.

On the tenth morning it rained. Yesterday afternoon had been cloudy, and the heavy rain had started at daybreak. Tree branches were whipping around in the fierce wind. The morning streets were barely lit. No one was out walking. He decided to stay in bed and wait until the rain stopped. He was aware of a familiar tiredness and stiffness in his shoulders. At home, this would be about the same time he'd be finishing work for the day, and his body would feel exactly as it did now. He was continually conscious of what time it was at home. He attempted to sleep a little longer, but the noise from a group of people in the dining room seeped through the wall.

Most of the tourists had stayed in this morning because of the rain. When he showed up in the dining room with his disheveled hair, the Chinese-looking man, who was with a group of tourists, stood up to prepare breakfast for him, and in a take-it-for-granted manner, also mentioned several galleries that could be visited on a day such as this. For whatever reason, he now understood the man's speech much better. Perhaps he'd gotten used to his pronunciation, or perhaps the man was speaking more clearly. He talked about one gallery that Baik was particularly fond of.

He stared intensely at the man, willing him to stop talking. The staring and the man's sudden silence alerted the foreigners in the dining room to something strange going on. Everyone stopped talking. The hostile atmosphere that filled the room was palpable. He couldn't endure it any longer and rose from his chair. The man stopped him from leaving and asked him to finish his breakfast. He shook off the man's arm and swore at him in the language of his own city. The foreigners didn't understand his language, but they were able to discern his mood from his face and his tone of voice. He was bewildered by his own anger and behavior. He felt pressured by the man's eyes, and without realizing what he was doing, suddenly grabbed him by the collar. The man's face turned red. He tightened his grip, and then realized he was disturbing the group's informal gathering.

One of the foreigners intervened and forced him away from the Chinese-looking man, who gave him a nasty look and left the dining room. He stared blankly at the door through which the man disappeared. The angry foreigners passed roughly by him, and he was pushed outside. The rain had at last let up, although the wind was still fierce. He pulled his clothes tightly around him, but still felt the icy cold on his back. He left his schedule and Baik's excellently compiled guidebook in his lodging. If he'd taken them, he'd only have thrown them in a trash can.

He walked and walked. When he was hungry, he randomly chose a restaurant. Every so often, he realized he was spending his time as he pleased for the first time. He wasn't dependent on Baik. Other times, he looked into his wallet to see how much he had spent, as though he'd been taking out loans. He looked at his watch time and again as if he was checking his bankbook and waiting for money to be transferred. This holiday of his had consisted of nothing but continual jaunts—all of them boring, haphazard, and meaningless. He felt deeply sad that he was so unable to enjoy anything sincerely. Bit by bit, he started to suspect that he'd been robbed by the city's infamous gypsies. He couldn't stop worrying that some of his important possessions had been stolen and frequently groped around in his clothing for his wallet and other possessions to make sure they were there.

It wasn't until he started thinking about returning to his lodgings that he became fully aware that he'd arbitrarily boarded a bus, gone on walking in all different directions, and didn't know his exact address. He was lost. At first he was embarrassed. But then he told himself that it wasn't unusual for a tourist to be lost, and considering that it was only a few hours since he'd left, he thought, he couldn't have wandered very far.

He started looking at the bronze panels on the buildings. The alleys were all so similar to each other. The store names and items displayed in the small shop windows all began to look the same to him. He passed through alleys that intertwined like veins along the road. Some alleys had houses with dim lights in their windows. He followed one alley for a while, then turned back. He walked up another alley and came back down again. He repeated this over and over. Then he found an alley that looked familiar. It looked like his alley, and he took it without hesitation. It was a long while before he realized he was wrong again and turned around. Then he realized that he'd wandered down the same alley several times already, and burst out laughing. At the end of it, he ran into a man in a hat leaning against a wall, smoking. Then he saw the same smoker a second time. After trying his luck down several more alleys, he found himself back yet again in the same place, staring at the cigarette butts the smoker had left on the ground. They seemed something like stars in a cloudy sky, lying there in that alley of shuttered stores and dim, useless streetlights.

As he wandered the streets, he remembered a newspaper article he'd read some time before. Based on a cell phone company's survey, designed to improve their navigation system, the article listed cities throughout the world in which the largest number of tourists got lost. This city was number one. The statistics showed that one out of every ten people lost their way on these streets. He looked enviously at the passersby—those nine out of ten people who did know their way. He watched them walk down the dark, narrow, redbrick alleys without having to turn around even once. He couldn't imagine how they found their way in these so nearly identical streets. Staring blankly around him, he wondered if he was the only one going in and out from one alley to another. Perhaps some of these passersby were also lost. At least some of them must be complaining about the maze-like paths and wandering around the mouths of strange alleys. He thought about the one out of every ten, roaming about as he was, and pitifully, he observed the dim streetlights, the dim round circles of light they cast, and the dark alleys that finally all looked the same.

But he wasn't yet completely hopeless. He hit upon a simple solution for locating his lodgings. He didn't want to call Baik, but he thought if he did, he could get the address, write it down, and show it to a taxi driver. That would solve his problem. Baik had said that he kept his cell phone turned on even when he was sleeping, so there was no question he'd answer. After talking with Baik, he could hail a cab and get back to his lodgings. It would be as simple as that. But since he'd done so much more walking than usual that day, he was hungry, and he decided first he'd go to a restaurant. He had some slight hope that eating good food might help him remember the address.

He checked out a few restaurants. In some, he saw very few locals, which suggested the food wasn't especially good. In others, the food might have been better, but the prices were too high. Still others were just too crowded. He soon tired of the whole process, finally settled on a restaurant, and ordered one of their most expensive dishes. This place seemed to be a combination of all the others that he'd already investigated. It had few customers and, considering the quality of the food, was far too expensive. But at this point, he felt he had little choice. His steak was too big, almost raw, and very tough. Chewing it was a major project. Then unexpectedly, as he was eating, he thought he remembered his street name and number. He wasn't completely certain, but he felt he was remembering it because he'd studied the bronze panel long enough to have memorized it. He decided to rely on his memory and go looking for the address. Dropping his fork and napkin, he hurriedly left the restaurant.

He stopped a passerby at random and asked for directions. The passerby took a long time trying to explain in the local language. Then, realizing this wasn't working, he stretched out his arm, pointing first left and then right, and using his fingers to indicate how many houses it was beyond the mouth of the alley. He did his best to express his appreciation for the stranger's kindness, carefully followed the directions, and came to a small park surrounded by a group of apartments. He turned back, checking to see if he'd taken the proper left and right turns. But it was no use. He asked another passerby, who pointed in a different direction. He walked for a long time following the new directions, and once again arrived at the small park. He had come through a different entrance, but it was the same park he'd reached before. He realized then that all the alleys he'd followed, one after another, were elements of a maze that radiated from this central point.

Occasionally, he heard a cat crying off in the bushes, but he saw no sign of human life. There were a few lights coming from the little old apartments, but they were as dim as the moonlight and did little to light up the park. In one corner, he discovered an old slide, some chin-up bars, and a jungle gym with fading paint. He leaned against the jungle gym, which cast a faint shadow on the ground. Some of the bars had been worn shiny by children's play. He hung on the lowest one and his feet touched the ground, even when he bent his knees. He was reminded of the second part of that same newspaper article, which explained that, in this city, one out of every three passersby would deliberately give visitors wrong directions, just for the fun of it. It was his bad luck to have met two of them, one right after the other.

Since there was no good place to sit, he sat astride the lowest bar of the jungle gym. He was uncomfortable on the cold thin bar with no support for his back, and he had to bend his head so as not to hit it on another bar. From this position he stared up to the top of the jungle gym. He'd always been afraid of heights, and only once in his life had he climbed all the way to the top of a jungle gym. His friends easily climbed up to the top even if they sometimes slipped. He was teased so much by these friends that one day he dried his sweaty palms on his pants and stepped up onto the first rung. He managed to climb up all seven tiers, but he derived no joy from his accomplishment. Looking down through the colorful iron bars he could see the hard, yellowish earth far below. Terrified, he started down, lost his footing and slid, badly injuring his head and arms. He could never understand why such a thing as a jungle gym should ever be allowed on a children's playground. One of the things he appreciated most about being an adult was that he was no longer under peer pressure to do things that frightened him.

Methodically, he adjusted his clothes and made his way across the park. He felt better now that there was nothing more he had to climb. But, then again, he also felt like a little boy who was just starting to climb a jungle gym. Or perhaps he felt that he'd already reached the top trembling with fear. He'd been thrown into a dull and dangerous game that he was compelled to play, and he found little joy in it because he was too afraid of being hurt. Yes, that was exactly how he felt.

He hurried away. Two out of three people in this city had to be willing to give him the right directions. Nine out of ten would know the way. If he was lucky, he'd meet the two out of three and become one of those nine out of ten. The alleys were dark, but he had to keep going. He had to move. He started walking down an alley—an alley he might have walked down before.

ROOM WITH A BEIGE SOFA

JIN, A THIN MAN, looked nervously down the local road. The field of tall grass shivered in the wind. Twenty steps away from him, his wife, Seo, held their hundred-day-old baby in her arms. They could see a vast rice field and a beat-up old black car in the distance. Driving along, Jin had seen fewer and fewer houses. Now there was only a field and a few cars passing, stirring up a cloud of dry dust that made him cough.

He'd had to brake suddenly when an animal, a roe deer, suddenly appeared out of nowhere. The abrupt stop had frightened Seo. She'd jumped in her seat and screamed. The baby woke up, and when Seo got out of the car to calm the crying child, Jin got out too. He was afraid the animal would come back and threaten his wife and baby. It occurred to him that it might have been just a dog or a cat, but he thought it was a roe deer—a tall, hopping creature that had jumped out into the road. He'd heard that many animals ran helter-skelter out into the road and were killed, but whatever animal he'd seen had vanished.

He sensed movement in the tall grass, felt tension in his feet. He reacted to the slightest sound. He was ready to drive away the moment an animal appeared. But if it turned out to be a huge animal, something other than a roe deer, he knew he'd have to run to Seo and the baby instead. With this in mind, he kept a close watch on his wife.

It was humid, actually too humid for the beginning of June. It looked as though there'd be a downpour any moment. Seo tucked up her long sleeves but continued to perspire. Her wet black hair was sticking to her forehead. The perspiration on her chest revealed the outline of her underwear, and the infant in her arms was fretful. She sang a lullaby over and over without stopping. The baby was always peevish when tired, and had to be soothed in her arms for some time before falling asleep. Seo continued rocking and singing. She looked like a peasant woman. She called out to Jin, but her voice was swept away by the sound of a swiftly passing car. She waved her hands at him, and he understood that she wanted to get going.

They were on their way to Seoul, moving there after eight years in a small city. Jin started to yawn and, at just that moment, a fly flew into his open mouth. Making a loud noise, he hawked and spit out the phlegm.

"I hope it rains," Seo sighed in a soft voice, looking up at the sky.

"A day like this won't give us much relief," Jin replied.

Before starting the car, he turned to look at the tall grass once more. He was curious. Had it really been a roe deer? Where did it go? It came to him that nothing at all had blocked his way. The grass thicket shivered in the gusting wind. There was nothing else out there. He remembered that he'd been tired and had briefly dozed off. It was possible that he'd seen a phantom. Nothing, absolutely nothing, had been there to disappear. Yet he still had a vague sense of something that had been left behind him. He fixed his eyes on the road ahead, resolving never to see a dark phantom again. Then, without warning, something hit his windshield and blurred his sight. A sudden rain. He grabbed a towel and wiped the windshield, tossed the towel down on the seat next to him, and turned on the ignition. The car started right away, but the wipers didn't budge. He turned them off and on again. The rain fell harder, obscuring his view of the road ahead.

"Are they broken?" Seo asked, as their baby began to cry peevishly.

"It seems they are," Jin replied, feeling utterly hopeless.

If only this were happening any other time than now, he thought. As far as Jin was concerned, a car was merely a black blob of machinery whose inner workings he didn't understand. He'd never repaired a car himself. He was always able to find someone around who could help him with any minor problems, or he simply went to a nearby car center. The mechanics did it all, changed the oil, changed the tires, and replaced fuses for him. The rain began to hammer the car more fiercely. He had no choice but to hurry and get off this local road.

"Why did you take this road anyway?" Seo asked, anxiously.

"You don't know why?" Jin bluntly replied.

"I didn't know it was such a narrow road," Seo said.

"Neither did I. This is my first time on it too, but they say it's a shortcut."

Seo looked at the baby, who wouldn't go to sleep unless she soothed it while she was standing up. This meant that she had to get out of the car every so often. Which was why they'd chosen the local road.

"I wish we could find a gas station," Jin muttered. He could barely see outside at all now through the hard rain.

"On a narrow road like this, we are never going to find a gas station," Seo gloomily responded.

Picking his way along like a blind man, Jin drove the car for twenty-some minutes before he finally spotted a gas station sign. He and Seo laughed. They'd expected neither the rain nor the gas station. Now here they were, and there was nothing more to worry about except the baby's incessant crying.

Only as they came closer to the gas station did they realize that their car trouble wasn't going to be solved after all. The fuel pump at the gas station was turned off. The waterproof covering over the pump was white with accumulated dust. The damaged front door to the office stood open. The front of the beverage vending machine was broken and rattling in the wind, and the roof that had once sheltered the whole place now barely covered the fuel pumps.

Jin was about to turn and leave, when he saw someone pacing inside the dilapidated building. He thought it wouldn't hurt to go in and ask for help. He parked the car and ran to get under what was left of the roof. In the barren office, several young guys were drinking. They stared at him, not speaking as he barged in. Jin took note of their reddened eyes and the strong smell of alcohol. He was also aware of a strange, fishy odor. It was something he'd smelled somewhere before, but he couldn't remember what it was. He only knew it was strong and that it gave him a headache.

"Not around here. You have to go farther up," one of the guys replied, when Jin asked if there was a car center nearby.

He wasn't going to bother them anymore, but then he changed his mind and asked the guy if he could handle car trouble. The cocky young man rose up from his seat, and looked around at the other drinkers, who gave him a thumbs-up.

He and Jin soon became thoroughly soaked looking under the hood of the car. The guy was wearing a clay-colored tee shirt with a picture of two tigers printed on it. Every time he took a breath, the tigers looked as though they were growling on his chest. Jin stared at them. When the guy lifted his head, raindrops rolled down onto his chest, and the tigers appeared to be drooling. The wipers still weren't budging.

"Do you know what the problem is?" Jin asked.

"Just the usual sort of problem. The fuse might have burnt out or something like that," the guy replied, glancing at Seo in the car feeding her baby.

"I really don't know much about cars, so..." Jin began, and the guy, seeming annoyed, slowly opened the hood again.

For some time, Jin watched him tinkering with the complicated machinery. Then he went and stood under the roof. A white cloud of cigarette smoke from the guys inside drifted out and surrounded him. He couldn't hear very much of what they were saying because of the wind, but he surmised they were telling dirty jokes. He knew about the young men of this region. It was the area near the small city where he'd worked for the past eight years. They had a peculiar tone of voice and used words that differed from the standard language. They spoke so aggressively that the difference between argument and joke was indistinct. They were frequently misunderstood, and conversations with them often ended in fights.

After graduating from poor schools, these young men had only two choices. They could either leave the region, or stay. There were several reasons for them to leave for good. The young men who stayed worked as laborers at a large shipping company. Those who didn't work as laborers earned their living by running dining, drinking, or entertainment establishments for the laborers. There was also a crowd of no-good rascals who were just hanging around waiting to leave town. Jin thought the guy in the tiger print tee shirt and his gang of heavy smokers belonged to this group, and he knew he shouldn't expect much of anything from them.

He didn't move, however. The storm had darkened the sky, and he knew that without working windshield wipers in these weather conditions, he could easily run off the road and into a field. The young guy leaned under the hood again and kept his head close to the unfathomable machinery. But every so often he turned to look at Seo, whose breast was in full view. With her small white face, she could easily have been mistaken for a young virgin if she hadn't been holding a baby. In fact, there was a fairly large age difference between Jin and Seo, and she was probably closer in age to the young guy. Jin wasn't at all pleased with her nursing her baby in front of him.

"All done. It wasn't as simple as it looked," the young guy said. Jin leaned into the car and turned on the wipers. They moved at a normal rhythm. He thanked the guy and opened the car door.

"You're not leaving just like that, are you?" the guy asked, smiling innocently, a smile incongruous with the tigers on his chest. He made a round circle with his thumb and index finger together. "I thought you'd at least express your gratitude."

Jin apologized. He felt embarrassed that he hadn't been able to tell the difference between a favor and a business transaction. The guy glanced back at the building. One of his buddies, a guy with a short haircut, waved to him, and he immediately ran in that direction. Jin took his wallet out of his jacket pocket. He decided to hand over some money to "express his gratitude" and tried to figure out how much he should pay. He pulled out three ten-thousand-won bills. Seo stared blankly at him. The baby sucked her last drops of milk. He hesitated and put one of the bills back in his wallet. Two bills, he thought, would have been what he'd have paid at a car center.

Jin walked into the office. The strange odor, either because of the rain or because of the dilapidated building, struck him as being even stronger than before. It occurred to him that it wasn't just cigarette smoke—that perhaps it was pot. He'd once watched a news program that showed marijuana growing along the local state roads, planted in among the grass where it blended in well. The marijuana he saw on the TV screen had looked like common grass, but with saw-like leaves and straw-like stems.

Jin put the money in the guy's hand. The guy unfolded the two bills and shook them before Jin went back out through the broken door. Walking quickly, Jin wondered if he'd shown enough appreciation with the amount he'd offered. Before getting into the car, he looked back at the guy through the broken window. He caught some of the other guys' eyes. They were staring at him, blowing smoke and pretending to pout like they were making fun of him. The guy who repaired the wipers was holding the money between his teeth and cupping his hands over the two tigers. Jin supposed the guy was making circles on his chest to suggest breasts. Jin was angry with him, but also with Seo. He couldn't understand why she'd had to nurse the baby at that particular moment. He felt that she smiled too easily and was too friendly with other men.

"Take good care of her," those who saw Jin's young wife would say. Jin knew this was an exaggerated joke referring to the age difference between them, but he got upset when they made such jokes, which insinuated he was a filthy old man.

Seo had been a contract worker in the branch company, and Jin was attracted to her mostly because she didn't speak with a strong local accent. Unlike others from that region whose voices sounded so aggressive, Seo's voice was soft and tender. He liked the way she tried to hide her peculiar regional accent. When he was living alone in company housing, he thought he might have to go to Vietnam or northern China to find a bride. He knew that if Seo rejected him, it wouldn't be the end of the world. Vietnam and China would still have plenty of candidates.

However, although it took a long time, Seo eventually accepted his proposal, and he felt lucky not to have to teach a foreign woman his language just so they could communicate with each other.

"Is everything all right now?" Seo asked, and Jin, who was irritated, shouted at her to pull up her blouse.

He was about to drive off when he saw the young guy standing in front of his car with rain dripping off his head. Jin hesitated a moment, wondering whether he should get out of the car or just keep going. He rolled down the window.

"You might have had an accident if you kept driving with broken wipers in this weather," the guy shouted through the rain.

"I thought what I gave you was enough," Jin muttered, but he was prepared to give the guy more, if he asked for it.

"It depends," the guy said and pushed his arm in through the open window. He grabbed Jin by the collar. "It might be enough, but the thing is, we helped you out. We didn't just do some simple errand for you. And hey, we're not twelve-year olds going out to buy candy with your petty change."

Jin realized that these guys, while longing to leave for some other place, were scared, insecure, and self-destructive, and therefore criminally inclined. They were afraid of being controlled or hurt, so they threatened others. Individually they weren't dangerous, but in groups they were often aggressive. He wanted to handle this situation as delicately as possible. He was, after all, leaving this town for good. He resolved never to come back to this road again, not even in his dreams.

He glanced at Seo and the baby in the rearview mirror. The peevish baby calmed down for a moment and moved its mouth, as if waiting for his decision. Seo looked back and forth between Jin and the young guy. Up to this moment, Jin had lived his life not exactly courageously, but always managing to avoid situations that would have made him appear cowardly.

"Instead of doing this," Jin said, gently taking hold of the guy's hand, "you might tell me how much appreciation I can show you."

Smiling, the guy let go of Jin's collar, and Jin opened his wallet and showed it to him. He'd filled his wallet with paper money to pay for the moving company and any other unexpected expenses.

The guy haphazardly yanked a wad of money out of the wallet and said: "This is the way to show your appreciation."

Jin had no idea how much he had taken. But that money was going to be spent by that evening anyway, he thought. The guy knocked at the window, tuk tuk, as if saying goodbye. Then, as if nothing had happened, he returned to the group to continue smoking cigarettes or marijuana, drinking, sharing dirty jokes, and occasionally indulging in blackmail.

Jin started the car and hurriedly peeled away from the gas station. He held his breath until it was out of sight. Then he exhaled. The baby once more grew sleepy and fretful. Listening to the peevish baby, Jin stopped the car and pulled out his cell phone.

"Why don't you just keep on going?" Seo urged.

"I'm calling the police," he replied.

He didn't really want to report the incident to the police. He and his family were on their way to another place for good. Soon they'd be there and there'd be no need to inform the police. Besides, calling them would only delay their arrival.

"What are you going to report? Are you going to say they took too much money for the repair? Or that they grabbed you by the collar?" Seo asked.

Jin didn't reply. He stared at the windshield. The storm had filled up the potholes scattered over the road. He'd already splashed his way through a few of them. He was about to hang up the phone and restart the car when a voice answered.

"Hello." Jin thought of the guy biting the paper money, drawing breasts on his chest and snickering while moving his stomach up and down to make the tigers look as if they were growling.

"What's the problem, sir?" the voice on the other end of the phone inquired, and Jin reported the guys to the police as marijuana smokers. He described them, including their clothing and the location of the gas station.

"What if that turns out to be wrong? Then what will you do?" Seo asked anxiously.

"I have no doubt about it. The smell was distinct, and did you see his eyes—the dilated pupils?"

Jin started the car. Whether it was true or not, it was reported, and they had no plans of ever returning to this town. There was no chance of their ever seeing those guys again. The wipers swept away the rain.

"That wasn't necessary. You shouldn't have done that. They were just drunk."

"We're on the road again, O.K.?" Jin turned around to glare at Seo. She turned away from him. He wanted to go faster. At this pace, they wouldn't get to the new house before the moving van arrived.

"Our moving van will be well on its way, I imagine," Seo said suddenly, when they noticed a truck overtaking their car.

"Of course," Jin replied.

Seo worried about the items they'd purchased for the new house. They'd been living in company housing that was completely furnished, and had had to buy almost everything needed for their new home. Each day, when he returned home from work, Jin would tell Seo what he'd ordered that day. He was indeed as thrilled as she was, but he tried to hide his excitement by asking her every so often not to waste money on unnecessary items.

Since Seo was about to leave the city that was her hometown, she tried to console herself by purchasing new furniture and appliances. First, she chose a colorful refrigerator with an icemaker that she thought would be useful. She bought a standing air-conditioner the same color as the refrigerator, as well as a new style of washing machine with special functions for washing blankets and sanitizing the laundry, and she was pleased when she received a microwave as a bonus item. But the most elaborate item she purchased was a sofa.

The one in their company housing was old and squeaky. They could feel the springs when they sat on the broken seats, and the disintegrating sponge protruded through the tattered cover. Since the furniture belonged to the company, they couldn't discard it. They wanted to have it repaired, but the property management personnel told them to wait: the person in charge wasn't available. So Seo had to sit on the floor holding her baby. She complained about back pain, and they both felt depressed living with that dark sofa and its worn-out upholstery that revealed the spiral outlines of its springs. The sofa was a symbol of their cramped, tiresome life in company housing tucked away in a small city.

Seo went to furniture store after furniture store in search of a sofa she really liked. She changed buses many times and went beyond the border of the province to go to a furniture mall. Finally, she chose a beige sofa designed for a four-member family. The leather upholstery was strong but soft. It looked like the delicious layers of a freshly baked pie, and seemed it couldn't possibly contain any spiral shaped springs, nailed wood, or cheap sponge.

The sofa had been delivered to their company housing before they moved, and it was a difficult task for their moving men since it was too large to get into the elevator. Wobbling and bumping against the walls, while the four moving men carried it down seven floors, this beige sofa was to represent Jin and Seo's new life. Jin eagerly tried to help them. He held on tightly to the vinyl wrapped around the sofa and lifted with all his might. He wanted a pristine sofa with no marks or scars to begin his new life.

After the sofa was loaded onto the truck, he rubbed his throbbing arms. He was no longer young enough to handle such a heavy weight. He'd spent most of his time working at the branch among the ship builders' hammers and the welders' flames. The loud noises that assaulted his ears were the result of work being done for the sole purpose of producing assembly-line items or for drying various parts of a ship. The hammering sounds lingered in his ears and pounded in his head. Sometimes, working at the branch, he felt that his whole life was an assembly-line item that the workers had made, destined to become a small part of a huge ship. Now, as he was leaving, he was reminded of scenes from his life as a young company man, and realized to his great relief, that he had outgrown them forever. He'd had the life of a young man that had gradually been consumed by greeting his superiors and keeping himself busy with various trivialities while awaiting his promotion.

Before his marriage, he spent his holidays and weekends alone in company housing. Sometimes he had night work, but generally he left the office early. Returning home, he'd first turn on the television, which was tuned to a twenty-four hour news channel that he never changed. Lying down facing the television, he'd watch whatever news came on. On weekends he watched television from early evening until he fell asleep. That he felt bored once in a while didn't really trouble him.

He didn't socialize much with his colleagues. They'd stop talking when he approached, or they'd change the topic to one that Jin knew nothing about. At regular departmental dinner parties, they seemed to get together separately after Jin left. He maintained an official relationship with them solely for business purposes. Jin thought this was simply because he was a manager. But later he discovered that other managers in the same region had comfortably good relationships with their workers. He didn't have much social contact with his colleagues at the central office either. The central office workers weren't particularly friendly with those from the regional branches. They preferred to socialize within their own exclusive group. Jin wasn't even a manager then, but he'd felt awkward whenever he attempted to join their conversations.

Nonetheless, during the past eight years, he'd been missing his life in Seoul. Many nights mindlessly watching television in company housing, he remembered drinking cold beer with his central office colleagues. Although he rarely attended them, he remembered that often when work was finished in the factory and the whole city calmed down in early evening, there would be dinner parties at noisy entertainment venues in the city. When his work was boring and he felt left out by his colleagues, Jin reminded himself that this dispatched position, which required him to live in this region, was only a temporary assignment. Someday he'd return to Seoul. Like most of the workers, although not born in Seoul, he thought of it as his hometown. He'd left the city only temporarily with hopes of going back soon. He'd never leave Seoul for good.

He had volunteered to work at the remote branch, though in fact he'd had no other option, since it was likely that he'd have had to accept an honorary retirement at a relatively young age if he hadn't volunteered.

"Once you are dispatched to a branch office, that's it. You never know when you'll return," his boss had told him when he announced that he'd decided to leave for the branch.

Jin realized this.

"But isn't it extraordinary that I don't have to quit the company right now?" Jin had asked.

This boss, who'd advised him not to leave for the branch eight years ago, was no longer with the company. He hadn't been promoted, and he resigned when he reached the limit of his term as a department manager. It was usually more difficult for a company man to be made a director of the company than it was to be promoted from a branch office to the central office. Jin heard that this former boss of his now ran a franchise restaurant somewhere. If he'd remained with the company, he'd probably once again advise Jin that he shouldn't expect to be promoted beyond the position of department manager. Then Jin would nod and reply, almost as before: "But isn't it extraordinary that I am now being promoted to the central office?"

He had driven a short way, when the car suddenly stopped. He tried everything he could think of, but it wouldn't budge. The windshield wipers efficiently swept back and forth as though ridiculing him. He turned the emergency lights on and got out of the car. The rain had let up somewhat, but it was still fairly heavy. He heard a distant siren. Certainly it must be the police coming to arrest those guys. He hoped they were indeed marijuana smokers. Even if they weren't, he couldn't feel sorry for them. Being taken to the police station to give blood and urine samples wouldn't cause them all that much trouble.

Jin opened the hood. The rain fell onto the block of black machinery. He was convinced that he'd been tricked by the young guy who repaired one thing and deliberately damaged something else. He resented having lost money to such a criminal. Grumbling, he phoned the insurance company. He decided to just watch the rain while he waited for the insurance man to arrive. It would probably turn out to be around the time that

Seo and the baby would wake up. By then, he'd be bored with the scenery, the car would be repaired, and they would go on to arrive safely at their new home. He could hear the siren. It sounded closer, then farther away again, until for a long time he couldn't hear it at all. He heard it once more after that, and then it faded away completely. He stared out into the distance to where the sound had disappeared.

He phoned the moving van driver who told him they were near the tollgate exit into Seoul. Jin reminded him that their things should be handled with care.

"Yes, yes, this is my tenth year driving a moving van on the road. You don't need to worry," the driver said, but his cheerful reply didn't persuade Jin. After once more urging the driver to take good care of their furnishings, he hung up. If he'd known the van would arrive at the house ahead of him, he'd have drawn a detailed map for the workers to show them how the furniture should be arranged. But now there was nothing he could do. The current situation couldn't have been predicted any more than the potholes that had suddenly appeared on the road. Some of them would merely splash water over the car, but others could cause the wheels to sink deep into the mud. So far Jin had encountered only the shallower ones.

Time passed. Jin dozed, until the ringing cell phone woke him. He picked up the phone quickly so it wouldn't wake Seo and the baby, who were still sleeping. It was the moving van driver calling to inform him that they'd just arrived at his new house. The moving date had been specifically selected for a day when there would be less traffic on the expressway and the local road. The traffic was light, as predicted, and he and Seo should have long ago arrived. Jin had envisioned them entering their new home together and looking forward to their future. It bothered him to know that the moving men would go into the house before them and walk around the place in their muddy shoes.

"You found a good house. The surroundings look fantastic," was the moving man's polite greeting. This didn't, however, especially please Jin. He asked them to start arranging the furniture, saying:

"We are actually having some car trouble."

"Sorry to hear that. So it'll take you a while to get here," the moving man replied, in a worried tone. But Jin worried that it was the workers who might take their time, knowing that the owner wouldn't be quick to arrive.

"The insurance man is here and we're working on the car now," he said. Seo woke up and was staring at him. "It will take us only about thirty minutes to get to Seoul. I can see the bright lights of Seoul from here," Jin said.

The moving man told him they'd start to arrange the furniture, and he hung up.

Jin stretched and got out of the car. He retrieved a large umbrella from the trunk. The rain was letting up. He looked back toward the region they'd left and saw the shadowy figures of several chimneys on the horizon. He knew that under those chimneys were several huge factory buildings as solid as ships. He remembered the pipes, the iron stairways, and the fuel tanks that could be seen from the outside. All of it felt somewhat strange and raw to him. He was used to the clean-cut, square shapes of skyscrapers.

He turned in the direction of their destination. From where he stood, Seoul wasn't visible at all. Thick layers of overlapping mountains peacefully blocked a view of the city. The scenery made Jin realize that, having left the world of noisy hammers and the sparks and flames of welders' tools behind him, he was now about to enter a world of uncertainty but also a world with solid and well-organized documents.

To reach this place, a person had to follow an endless road through a field sparsely populated with houses, past a vast fog-enshrouded lake lined with motels, and drive all the way through a newly established apartment complex. But just to know that Seoul was there made Jin feel reassured. It was in Seoul that he'd been a student, from elementary school through to college. There, on a playground, he'd experienced his first shy love, his first kiss. There that he and his brothers and sisters cried when their parents passed away.

The darkening roadway, the endless field, the immobile car, and the sudden storm made Jin anxious again, and aware once more that he was still far from this familiar world. The ringing phone made him more anxious still.

It was the moving man again, not the insurance company returning his call.

"Good God! We should change insurance companies, or do something," Jin muttered as he answered the phone.

"Did you measure the space before you chose your sofa?" the moving man asked loudly. "It doesn't fit in your living room."

Jin remembered the first time the real estate agent took him to see the house. It was somewhat disorderly, but it projected a warm, comfortable and sophisticated atmosphere. Looking around, Jin tried to determine what made it feel this way. There was a master bedroom with a queen-size bed, a full-sized wardrobe, and a dressing table. The kitchen had a highly polished kitchen sink. There was a dark-colored dining table for four. There was a desk and a bookshelf with randomly shelved books. All these items could commonly be seen in any home. But when he noticed the large beige sofa on the left side of the living room, he understood where the special feeling came from.

The children who were on the sofa slowly sat up with their eyes fixed on the television screen as their mother admonished them to properly greet their guests. The sofa looked like a soft blanket that warmly caressed one's body. It was entirely different from the dark one Jin and Seo had in company housing. Compared to their old sofa that squeaked, revealed its sponge stuffing, and caused back pain, this beige sofa represented an immaculate and comfortable world far removed from broken springs and the smell of cheap sponge. Jin pictured his own family, his own children, peacefully sitting on such a sofa in the near future. Perhaps that was why Seo had chosen a beige sofa.

Jin handed the phone to her now, and she asked the moving man to place the sofa tightly against the left wall of the living room. In a few minutes, the phone rang again.

"I'm sorry but the sofa doesn't fit there. We've tried everything, but it doesn't fit."

It was because of the refrigerator, the moving man told her. The kitchen was too small and the refrigerator had to be placed on the wall that was shared with the living room. "We will just leave it askance for now. You can adjust it when you come."

Seo hung up almost in tears. When she was nervous or angry she couldn't hide her accent, and Jin couldn't bear to listen to her pleading in her native regional voice. He called the insurance company again. He too became disheartened, thinking about the beige sofa deposited at a weird angle in their living room. The insurance company repeated that their man had already left. But the insurance man, whom they said had left, didn't respond to Jin's call. He had no choice but to wait.

Meanwhile, the evening had become darker and darker. The road to Seoul had grown so dim that cars were disappearing in the darkness at the end of it. While Jin went on staring blankly at the road, the moving man continued calling Seo.

Where would you like your dining table? Your bookshelf? Your desk? Your dresser? He asked if she wanted items placed by a window or whether she'd like them in a corner, the left corner or the right corner, or underneath a window, and so on. He asked her for these details, and she calmly answered each question. She was responding for the second time to the same question about whether she wanted the bed placed right under the window, in the corner, on the left-side wall, or the right-side wall, when Jin grabbed the phone from her.

"We'll be there soon. Please put everything as you wish. Just put them down approximately where you think they should be. The only thing we have to do there tonight is sleep. That's all."

"But it should be done…" the moving man started to object, and Jin interrupted him again.

"No, you don't need our instructions every inch of the way. You have worked as a moving man for a long time, right? You should know where things go. Household goods are pretty much the same, aren't they?" Jin yelled at him.

The attractive furnishings they'd so carefully selected had suddenly mutated into ordinary things, and he was angry about that. The moving man hung up without replying, and Jin called the insurance man. After a long time, the man answered and said that, due to a traffic jam, it would take a while for him to arrive and he hoped that Jin would understand. Jin said he did understand, but he called him again every two minutes. After a while, the man stopped answering his calls. Jin wished he had called a tow truck instead. But this was hindsight. There was no way he could have anticipated this situation.

After some time, the insurance man sent a text message saying he'd arrive in five minutes. Jin felt better. He got into the car and closed his eyes. In the cooler evening air, the baby was sleeping and Seo kept her eyes closed, as if she needed to rest. Jin heard a

car coming and he opened his eyes. He was convinced it was the
insurance man finally arriving. He'd been planning to express
his anger, but now he was just glad to hear the car approaching.

But it wasn't at all what he'd anticipated. A fierce, wild animal
was coming toward him in the dim light. It stopped, and Jin saw
the beast—the tiger. There was no way of escaping from its jaws.
He thought it bit him, but in fact he'd been hit by a hammer.
He felt a tremendous hot pain in his head. It was like he was
being forced under hot running water falling from somewhere
high above him. At first it felt cool, and then it was unbearably
painful. He thought he was being held upside down in a cauldron of hot water. Not that he'd been hit. As the pain subsided,
he felt his face swell like a balloon. Something was running over
his swollen face. He touched it, and knew that he hadn't been
bitten or burnt in hot water. He knew that he'd been hit with
something hard.

A telephone rang somewhere. Maybe it was the insurance
man. Maybe the moving man. They still had so many things to
move in. So many things that needed to be arranged. In the grip
of the pain, Jin actually laughed a little. He thought he'd been
driving so carefully, avoiding the potholes, and here he'd ended
up in a big fiery hot cauldron. He laughed at himself. He didn't
know that he'd already drowned even as he was congratulating
himself for having avoided the potholes. When he was done
laughing, for whatever reason, he seemed to remember having
had a similar experience a long time ago, and he was comforted
in the midst of his pain, which went on and on. This would turn
out just like it had before. He'd emerge from this pain and go
back to the world out there, as if nothing had happened. He'd
accept it as a crisis he'd been destined to experience. Only this
time he had to be hit in order to get through the crisis. The
moment would pass, as it had before, however endlessly long it

seemed. But the scar would vanish and the broken bone would heal. Someone started laughing. He couldn't tell whether it was the laugh of an animal or his own laughter. Or could it be Seo, frightened, or the baby crying?

He tried hard to recognize the sound and make up his mind where to go next. In one part of the invisible city there was an apartment building illuminated late into the night. There were furnishings to sustain their new lives, still wrapped, improperly placed, tossed about like trash. They'd have to live with the beige sofa not fitting in their living room. The crooked sofa was going to cause him throbbing pain. He tried to stay awake. Cars with red eyes passed by on the night road on their way into the dark city.

CANNING FACTORY

THE NEWS SPREAD like wildfire. The plant manager hadn't shown up for work. It was his first absence ever. The shrewd workers believed he must have been in some kind of accident because he'd always come to work earlier and gone home later than anyone else. Someone had once called him the janitor and since then all the workers continued to call him that. He'd started out working on the production line. At that time, like most of the other workers, he appreciated the machinery that made his job easier, but he never trusted it. He doubled the number of sampling inspections, rust inspections, and vacuum-level inspections. He relentlessly harangued others for wasting time simply staring at the cans while the machinery did all the work. He interrupted every step of the process by demanding accurate methods of measuring production. He harassed the female workers by fondling their breasts while straightening their nametags. He insulted them by making loud, brazen jokes about the size of their breasts. He was impetuous. He expressed anger before sorting out a situation and didn't apologize even when he was proven wrong. All of these stories emerged as the director of the company interviewed individual workers trying to determine what had caused the plant manager's absence. The stories weren't altogether believable, but it was always the plight of a plant manager to be criticized by someone or other.

Park, who had worked the late shift the night before the disappearance, said that when he refused to have a drink with him, the plant manager had abused him to his face, saying that young people were impudent, and had then stormed off home to his company housing.

"So, do you think he was so drunk last night that he passed out and is still in bed?" the director asked Park, obviously not believing this was the case.

Actually, the plant manager did drink every evening. In the mornings when he came in earlier than everyone else, he always smelled of alcohol. He was, so to speak, a devout alcoholic. Park didn't respond. He merely turned his head aside to make it appear as though he was pondering the question.

"By the way, why were you working last night?" the director asked.

There was no reason for Park to have worked last night. Although it wasn't the case in larger companies, the employees in this factory never worked more than the regular, nine-to-six working hours. The management was becoming increasingly aware that the recession might spread worldwide. Besides which an increasing number of voices were raising suspicions about processed food. Every so often, just when these criticisms were about to fade from memory, some consumer would find an impurity, such as a knife blade, a thorny-headed worm, a shred of vinyl, or pieces of fingernails in a can. When this news was broadcast, domestic consumption decreased, sales plummeted, and the company had to rely on exports to stay in business. Then, to make matters even worse, the low price stratagems of neighboring countries also hurt them.

"It was the plant manager's personal request," Park finally replied.

"Personal request! Possibly you've forgotten this is a company. We don't pay you to conduct personal business."

"I canned," Park quickly responded.

"Aha, so you've just figured out what my company produces, eh? Here we only can, the same as yesterday, the day before yesterday, and twenty-three years ago. Today and tomorrow and twenty-three years from now it will be the same. We will can!"

"He said he was going to send them to T country," Park said. The director stared at him wondering what export items were produced for T country.

"The plant manager's daughter is taking a language course in T country."

"Is that so," the director nodded, and Park noticed that he was clenching his fists as though he wanted to break something. "That b...! Very well!" the director muttered. He knew exactly what kinds of cans were sent to one's child. Some time ago, he had sent them himself. When his son was studying in U country, he regularly had food sealed in airtight cans and sent them to him. Fresh kimchi and well fermented radish kimchi, seasoned raw crab dipped in soy sauce, marinated barbecue ribs and *Bulgogi* meat prepared to be broiled, and stir-fried small octopus were all put into cans. So were *Sikhye*, kimchi stew, curled mallow soybean soup, and stir-fried anchovies. During his study abroad, the director's son was never without food, and the director had had the plant manager do the canning for him.

Nevertheless, the plant manager had now acted as though he was the director and used the machinery for something other than company production. He had wasted the company's electricity and exceeded his authority by ordering an employee to work overtime. The angry director changed his mind. He didn't, as he'd planned, send Park to the company housing where the plant manager was living alone while his wife was in T country looking after their daughter, who was studying there. And when the plant manager didn't show up for work the next day or the day after that, the director vowed he'd never again let the plant manager step inside the company's door. He sent his secretary, the manager of general affairs, to the plant manager's house to notify him that he was fired.

At lunchtime, the workers from each section gathered in the lounge room and opened their cans of jackmackerel, mackerel, and seasoned sesame leaves to eat with the white rice they brought from home in their lunch boxes.

"This isn't the janitor's style," one of the workers said, chewing his mackerel.

What he meant was that the plant manager would have come to work earlier than anyone else even if he was so sick he was almost dying.

Someone else suggested that even though it wasn't as if something horrible had happened to him, perhaps his absence should be reported to the police. As though agreeing, they all nodded their heads while chewing their rice along with one of the canned foods—jackmackerel, mackerel, or seasoned sesame leaves.

"This reminds me of the janitor," another worker said, pointing at the open cans. The plant manager had always eaten breakfast alone at his place, a lunch of canned food with the workers in the lounge room, and some canned food again, as side dishes, during his evening drinking.

"Why did he live like that?" yet another worker asked, chewing a lump of rice wrapped in a sesame leaf.

"Who wouldn't live like that?" someone else responded, with the smell of fish slipping into his words as he swallowed his rice. They all quietly put the succulent rice mixed with fish juice and meat in their mouths. They chewed unusually slowly. Little by little, it dawned on them how their manager had eaten this run-of-the-mill lunch every day, just like them. They felt their lives had become as predictable as the canned foods they were consuming. Perhaps it was because they worked so hard and were so obedient. They even felt that their futures had already passed them by, and that the future for the few really successful individuals among them would be no different from the manager's present. But no one wanted to say this aloud, to admit that this was true. They didn't like the plant manager, but then again, they couldn't really hate him. They merely disliked him for no particular reason that they could discern.

They concluded their meal with canned peaches and oranges for dessert. While chewing the soft peach flesh, they debated about who would be the best person to call the police. They glanced at Park, wondering what he was thinking. They were concerned about the difficult situation in which he might find himself, considering he was the last person to be seen with the plant manager. By this point almost everyone suspected that something horrible had happened to him.

But Park had an alibi. After last night's overtime work, he'd gone out to eat at his usual restaurant, where he happened to meet another worker and join him at his table for dinner. A popular soap opera was being shown on television, and Park asked the restaurant owner why the female protagonist was always so bad-tempered. He noted that the tendons on her neck were actually protruding. The female owner responded by going on at some length about the character in the show. Consequently, even though Park had been the last person to see the plant manager, this encounter at the restaurant absolved him from any suspicion of wrongdoing. The intoxicated plant manager could have had the bad luck to lose his footing and fallen into the river, or been robbed of his wallet and beaten nearly to death, or been struck by a hit-and-run driver and thrown someplace where his body lay still undiscovered. These were all things that might well have happened, things that might happen to anyone.

As the last piece of peach entered a worker's mouth, the manager of general affairs rushed into the lounge room. He caught his breath and drank some sweet juice from a peach can.

"You could cut your lips drinking that way, sir," someone said to the manager of general affairs.

"Nonsense! I've been drinking juice this way for more than a day or two. That's how I drank it yesterday, and the day before yesterday, and twelve years ago," he said, putting down the can. "The director filed a report of disappearance with the police."

They all gasped as though every last one of them had cut their lips on a can.

"The police replied that..." The manager finished off the rest of his juice. They waited for him to continue. "...it could be a simple case of running away from home. So we have to wait and see."

Having finished his report, he now drank some sweet juice out of an orange can. The workers joined in with him, drinking juice a little at a time, like they were sharing warm fish soup in a freezing cold climate. The last of them to finish held their empty cans aloft and clinked them, as if sounding the signal bell that meant the end of lunch break.

*

Park was in charge of the hermetic sealing team. Around the time the plant manager was appointed, Park had mainly been canning jackmackerel, except for a brief period when he canned mackerel. The person in charge could change the production line as he wished. When he grew tired of the fishy, salty smell and felt nauseous, he could move to the agricultural line to can oranges or peaches instead. When he got tired of the sweet fruit smell, he could move back to the fish. This was true in principle, but no person in charge had ever actually moved around that way.

It was the plant manager who paved the way. He'd been canning jackmackerel for twelve years—ever since entering the company, back when it was just getting started. As time went on, he caught himself thinking that anything long and thin was a jackmackerel. Even something like an ordinary ruler was beginning to look like a jackmackerel to him. This problem was the one and only reason he was considering quitting his job. So he went to see the director.

"I am absolutely sick of jackmackerel," he complained. "A change to mackerel might work for me." He mentioned mackerel quite naturally because he happened to like it. The director frowned at the strong odor emanating from the plant manager's work clothes.

"Well, if that's how you feel, switch to the mackerel cans. Why not? Other companies operate that way."

And for the next ten years he'd remained with the company and canned mackerel.

Immediately after the first director's funeral, the second director started to expand the production line. The factory that had been permeated with the salty, fishy, oily smell of mackerel and jackmackerel then became infused with the sweet fragrance of orange juice, peach juice, and citric acid. Employees worked night shifts more often, and the company hired additional workers. The newly appointed plant manager made a speech in which he told the workers to choose whichever flavor they wanted to work with. Flavor. It was like a new word, a word that meant you actually had a choice like the choice you had in the music or the movies that you preferred, except that, in this case of course, the choices were jackmackerel, mackerel, peaches or oranges.

Park chose mackerel. This had nothing to do with his preference or anything else in particular. He was simply tired of jackmackerel. Most of the workers made similar choices. Some, who'd been working on the jackmackerel line, chose the mackerel line and vice versa. However, to those who were accustomed to handling jackmackerels, mackerels felt too large to manage. For those who were accustomed to mackerels, jackmackerels were too thin and slippery to grasp hold of.

It wasn't long before it was all the same, whether you were canning jackmackerels or mackerels. The contents differed, but the process never did. The workers cut, removed the intestines, marinated, cooked, hermetically sealed, sterilized, cooled, and finally canned the fish. Transferring from one line to another made no difference to anyone. Park thought about it and realized that jackmackerel was, after all, exactly the right flavor for him because he preferred the familiar. He returned to his former line.

Various rumors attached themselves to the plant manager's sudden disappearance. It was said that he'd been having an affair with a female worker and, fearing that it might be revealed, he disappeared. According to another story, he was drunk every night and went to the female worker's house. Some people reported having seen the two of them dating on weekends, but this couldn't be confirmed as the suspected couple had only been glimpsed from a distance. The woman might have been some other female worker, or someone who resembled her, or a friend's wife whom he'd met by chance. It could even have been his own wife since it was prior to the time she left for T country.

These whispered rumors spread quickly, but few believed them. They seemed unlikely because the plant manager had a dark face, a balding head, a large stomach, and short legs. The shoulders of his navy blue working clothes were covered with dandruff. The greasy hair at the back of his neck was shaped like a duck's ass. His breath smelled fishy, or like sweets from a child's mouth. He was hardly the type of man with whom a woman would ever fall in love.

The female worker to whom the rumor alluded was taciturn, pale, and forbidding. The other female workers felt uncomfortable with her or disliked her because she looked different from them. The male workers also disliked her, as they felt she was arrogant and unfriendly. The rumor of the affair was only partially correct. The plant manager did go to see her at her place, but he went there infrequently. And it wasn't true that their affair started after his wife left for T country. They had actually started seeing each other before that but had stopped a long time ago. As for the woman, she refused to say anything at all about him. She might have known something or she might not have. She kept her business to herself.

But the rumor persisted, and the possibility of embezzlement was added to it. It was said that the plant manager had been under financial pressure ever since sending his child to T country. Those who were better informed knew very well that the amount of money usually mentioned in the rumor had never been present in the factory. Nevertheless, no one made any attempt to dispel the rumor.

"If I returned home, my husband wouldn't just suddenly appear," the plant manager's wife replied, when the manager of general affairs called to tell her about her husband's disappearance.

Their daughter, who had finished her language course, had recently entered the upper level foreign school in T country. Since it was the beginning of the semester, she couldn't miss classes. Her mother had to stay with her and couldn't come back home.

"They tell me that cases like this usually involve not merely a disappearance, but, sometimes, an unnatural death," the manager of general affairs said in an almost threatening tone.

The plant manager's wife sighed.

"Even if he is dead, what difference would it make?" her cold voice replied. "He wouldn't come back to life if I returned. Let me know when you find his body. Then I'll come."

As he hung up the phone, the manager of general affairs was reminded that his own wife had recently been insisting that they send their child to a language program abroad. He decided they should reconsider this. It might not be such a good idea.

The police didn't start their investigation until a week after the report was sent in. They discovered that the relationship between the plant manager and Park had soured. Someone reported that he'd overheard Park arguing with the manager in the changing room on the same day that he disappeared. A policeman called Park into a side room in the canning factory for questioning. He asked why he'd fought with the manager in the changing room, if the manager often asked him to do personal work for him at night, how long it took to process the cans that night, what kind of cans he'd processed, what he did after leaving the factory, if the plant manager exhibited any unusual behavior on other days, and what exactly was his relationship with the plant manager. Park answered all these questions. The policeman left the side room and headed for the storage room. Park followed him without being asked.

"What did you do with the cans you processed that night?"

"The next day I sent them to T country as I'd always done."

"So were cans frequently sealed for private use in this way?"

Park slowly shook his head. But in fact many of the workers had done some secret, private canning. One of the workers sealed a ring in a jackmackerel can and gave it to his girlfriend. He said she opened the lid and found the shiny ring on the silver bottom of the can, put it on her finger, and smiled. Another worker sealed inexpensive Christmas gifts in cans to give to his child. Concealed inside a pop-top peach can, there would be a simple pack of Lego blocks or some kind of robot that could transform itself into an airplane. Other items sealed in cans by the workers had included the deed for someone's first home and a letter from a departed lover.

Yet another worker hermetically sealed a cat for his parents who were suffering with neuralgia. He claimed that he'd bought the cat from a market although his fellow workers listening to his story believed that he'd simply picked up a street cat. He said he boiled it for a long time to make a thick broth, which he then hermetically sealed in a can along with the cut up flesh. That particular caper was discovered, and he had to write an apology. But the incident made all of the workers aware of the limitless possibilities for canning items. They heard that the director kept cash in a can instead of a safe deposit box. At the beginning of the year, when the previous year's accounting was being done, someone had seen the director putting a bundle of paper money into a can before turning on the compressor. It was said that the director who heard the rumor severely reproached the workers, but that only made them more suspicious.

Once, when they were sealing cans to send to T country, the plant manager asked Park: "And you, what've you done?"

"Pardon?"

"What have you canned, I mean."

Park had never canned anything unusual. He had nothing to seal to keep for himself and no one special to whom he wanted to send a privately sealed can.

"This is just between us," the manager said slowly and then continued. "Before my daughter went abroad to study, our dog died. She held onto that dead dog and cried and cried. It was summertime and soon it was going to smell, but she wouldn't let us bury the dead dog. One night, when she fell asleep holding it, I quietly took it from her and sealed it in a can. For a while she kept it in her room. In the beginning she'd hold the can and cry, but when we brought another dog into the house, she ignored the can, and I threw it into the sea." The plant manager put his finger to his lips. "That's a secret."

Park nodded. He saw a flicker of regret in the plant manager's eyes—regret that he had revealed his secret. Park listened quietly, trying to demonstrate that he wasn't a man prone to gossip. But then neither did he want to give the plant manager the impression that he wasn't interested in his story, so he asked if the dog had fit in the can.

"The largest container was just the right size. It was a small dog. I didn't have to cut it up. Possibly it should have been cut up." The manager knit his brows as if imagining the task. "But I couldn't dirty my hands with a dog," he said, looking at the creases in his palms as though making sure his hands were free of blood stains.

"Sometimes," he continued, "I think that when I die, my body should be cremated and my remains should be preserved in a can. I wouldn't like to have my body rotting in the soil of a graveyard or in a marble box in a cinerarium. All my life I've worked in a canning factory handling cans. Seeing the changes in canning materials and lid-opening methods, I've seen life become easier and easier. Seeing new canning products, new seasonings,

I've seen how people's tastes change. I've learned about the world through cans."

"It would be a disaster if the world becomes like an empty can," Park said and immediately realized what a stupid remark he'd made. He quickly suggested that ashes might be sealed in a can before being taken to the cinerarium. The plant manager stared at him without smiling.

Standing there facing him, Park thought that he and the plant manager were like migrating birds in different seasons incapable of communicating with each other. In any event, he wondered why the plant manager had told him this story out of the blue. If Park had asked what was going on with him, he'd probably have revealed more of his secrets. But Park asked nothing more. If he had, and the plant manager had responded, what weird ideas might have been brought to light? No one would ever know.

"A big can like this," the police investigator asked, tapping on a ten-kilogram can with his fingers. "Where would it usually go?"

"Large cans like that are usually for exports or other enterprises."

"You like cans, don't you?"

"No, not really. I rather dislike them."

This wasn't what the policeman expected to hear. He stared at Park.

"If that's true, how could you have worked for ten years in a canning factory, eating canned foods every day?"

"I hardly ever eat canned foods. I don't like their taste. That doesn't mean that I shouldn't work in a canning factory. There are some men who make sanitary pads that they don't use."

The policeman nodded.

"Then you really don't enjoy the work?"

"I'd guess it's like you with your work. Some parts of it are interesting but other parts are not, aren't they? It's the same for me."

"Of course, but what's so difficult for you with your canning job?"

"Once in a while cutting my hands on a can or a lid is really bothersome."

"If that's all, then you could say that the work isn't so bad."

"But the fishy and the salty odors are hard to bear. The oily smell is also unpleasant. These days I'm working on the hermetic sealing line, but for a little while I worked in the intestine cleaning area and back then I hated anything that was soft and mushy—even a woman's body. But more than anything..." He paused. The policeman, whose eyes had been focused on the ingredients written on the can, turned his attention to Park. "...it's the same routine over and over that's really hard. All day long the only thing I do is hermetic sealing. Other workers chop jackmackerel heads all day or pull the slippery intestines out of fish stomachs with their fingers. Some workers salt fish all day. Some pack cans into boxes and boxes into packages."

"Nothing special to note there. What's the fun part?"

Park felt as if he were taking an exam—something he hadn't experienced since finishing school a long time ago. He felt annoyed and oppressed by the policeman who seemed to be listening to him in a half-hearted sort of way. Park answered him sincerely.

"It's that the same work repeats itself continuously."

The policeman gazed at Park accusingly as if he'd just made a joke. But Park went on.

"We're here, all day long, watching the empty cans spinning on the belt. They spin constantly. We get dizzy. Flies buzz at our ears. We pick our ears and they're filled with blood clots. This isn't the kind of job where it's possible to think. Standing in front of the belt, holding ourselves always at the same angle, our bodies become part of the machinery. For some reason, that's satisfying, but we're not proud of it."

The policeman nodded blankly. Through this whole interrogation, he'd written nothing in his notebook. Now he snapped it closed and asked Park to take him to the plant manager's company housing unit. Park felt so oppressed by the policeman's confidence, he almost mentioned that one day, when they hadn't realized the conveyor belt was out of order, they let the cans run through to be sealed a second time. But instead, he swallowed his words and walked toward the plant manager's company housing.

The singles' housing units were austerely furnished and barely functional. They had a hard bed suitable for a long-term hospital patient, a desk and a bookcase made of pressed sawdust, an upholstered couch, and a dresser—all of which had probably been purchased by the management of the General Affairs Department. In the plant manager's apartment there were very few cooking utensils. There was water, rice, wine bottles, and a few leftover canned foods in plastic containers in the refrigerator. Each of the storage closets contained cans of jackmackerel, mackerel, seasoned sesame leaves, peaches, and oranges. There were also cans in the kitchen cabinet over the sink and in the row of three drawers located under the sink. The dresser in which they expected to find clothing held three more drawers full of cans.

"If this guy's got these cans stowed all over the place like this, I guess they must be edible after all," said the policeman.

Park selected one can from each of the different kinds of cans in the closet and handed them to the policeman.

"Please try them yourself."

"All right, but later, when the plant manager comes back, you have to keep this a secret," the policeman said.

"No need to keep it a secret. We all eat canned food both in the factory and at home. Cans are part of our salary."

"Your salary?" the policeman asked, and Park nodded.

"The factory is always in financial difficulty. The depression is getting worse and worse. According to the director, the situation is so bad that smaller canning factories may not survive. Besides, people don't trust cans these days because the expiration dates are so far in the future. People are uncomfortable with food that doesn't rot at the right speed. Canning involves killing live food and hermetically sealing it to maintain it in that state, but people are suspicious about whether that state can really be maintained. So, not enough cans are sold, and the workers are given them as part of their salary.

"So, if you don't like the canned foods, what do you do with them?"

"I don't eat them, but I have relatives in other cities who do."

The policeman nodded.

"These cans you gave me today, could you tell me what the expiration dates are?" the policeman asked, as they left company housing and headed back to the factory.

"It depends on the item. Usually it's between twenty-four and sixty months. The expiration dates are printed on the lids."

"Up to five years. You mean this food won't go bad for five years?"

"It's kind of an assumption. Prior to the expiration date it's assumed that the condition is perfectly maintained. Right after the expiration date, it's assumed that the condition has immediately broken down. At that point we discard them regardless."

The policeman shrugged his shoulders and got in his car. A few days later he called the director and reported that due to a lack of clues regarding the plant manager's disappearance, his investigation would be discontinued.

*

Everything went along fairly smoothly in the factory without the plant manager. Nothing out of the ordinary happened except for those few mishaps that would normally occur at a canning factory. The machinery continued to operate. The canned food was processed and delivered on time. When the bell rang for lunch break, everyone assembled in the lounge room as usual. They arranged themselves in a circle with cans of food in front of them. They were perplexed as they opened the cans because it seemed more like a testing process at the end of a production run than eating a meal. Once started, however, they ate mechanically, as if it were a part of their production work. None of them were particularly fond of the food, but no one expressed their likes or dislikes. They ate quietly.

Then one day one of the workers declared that he was sick of canned foods, and he prepared pork kimchi stew in the kitchen. But because it took some time to cook, the hungry workers lost their appetites. They blamed their loss of appetite on the noise of the machinery and the odors of the workplace. The following day, when they hurried to open the cans and eat the canned foods with rice, they recovered their appetites. They'd all become accustomed to the fishy and salty taste of the canned foods, and they were grateful for their dull, easy-to-please tastes. They were offered a limitless number of cans, devoured the fish and rice, and finished their meal with the peaches and oranges.

"Is it really all right that we eat from cans like this every day?" one worker asked, and another worker replied: "Since it's only for lunch, it's all right." It might have been all right if it had only been for lunch, but most of the workers ate the canned foods at other times as well. Returning home from work, they prepared

stew or a steamed dish with the jackmackerel and kimchi, or
they minced the jackmackerel to make seasoned soybean sauce
and ate mackerel with jackmackerel soybean sauce over it. One
worker lamented that he'd gone to a grocery store and uncon-
sciously put some jackmackerel and mackerel cans which had
been processed in their factory in his shopping basket. Others
shyly confessed that they had done the same thing, and someone else observed: "It looks like, no matter what anyone says,
we must eat this stuff."

This was on the same day that every news outlet was broadcasting a story about another factory, in which cans were found
containing spiny-headed worms. But in any case the workers
wouldn't have eaten the canned foods only out of a sense of duty.
They did so, as the now absent plant manager had said, because
they'd acquired a taste for them.

While the workers sat in their circle and ate their canned
foods, Park slipped into the side room in the storage area, quickly
ate his own food, and took a nap. The room reeked from the
mingled odors of phenol, acetic acid, motor oil, machine lubri-
cant, rubber piping, boots, fish intestines, and fruit peels. Perhaps
it was because of these smells that Park dreamed about working
in the factory. In the dream, he handled hermetic sealing. He
sealed a can with his finger in it, and then sealed an empty can
in another empty can in another empty can.

Once he'd dreamed that the plant manager gave him items
to be sealed one at a time. He sealed possible as well as impossible items, like the director's cash box and the director's head.
The plant manager gave him a dog with its four legs cut off and
a huge piece of bleached bone. When he asked how to put the
bone in a can, the plant manager pointed at a grain grinder that
could be used as a mill. Park didn't hesitate to go to the grinder.
He adjusted the grinding level and inserted the bleached bone.

Flour spewed out. He collected it and put it in a can. The can was then mixed in among a thousand others, and all of them looked alike.

The lunch break was short. When the signal bell rang, the workers left the lounge room and proceeded to each line—the jackmackerel line, the mackerel line, the sesame leaf line, the peach line, and the orange line. Standing in front of the continuously spinning belts, they cleaned jackmackerels and mackerels, peeled peaches and oranges, soaked them in edible hydrochloric acid, processed them with acetic acid, watched the lids being placed on top of the cans, and randomly selected cans for testing.

Occasionally, there were minor accidents. Once, at closing time, a female worker who was close to tears reported that she must have dropped the contact lens for her right eye into one of the cans.

"How did that happen?"

"I think because I was sleepy, and I rubbed my eyes."

"How come you didn't know about it until now?"

"I'd been feeling dizzy, watching the spinning belt, but I thought it was vertigo, not my eyesight."

She hadn't realized that she'd lost the lens until she was getting dressed in the changing room after the day's work was done. The vertigo she'd been experiencing all day was actually caused by her distorted eyesight rather than by dizziness. She searched everywhere for the lens but couldn't find it. She'd worked on over a thousand fruit cans that day. After the sanitization process, the newly produced cans stood in a row waiting to be packed into boxes. One of those cans standing along the wall contained the lens she had dropped. To find the fingernail size lens, over a thousand cans would have to be opened. Although it was possible to can the food again, it wouldn't be an easy job. Besides which, the airtight sealed cans would be contaminated immediately after being opened. They couldn't be resealed.

"Tomorrow morning tell us that you found the lost lens," Park told the upset woman. "Tell us that the lens was stuck to your work clothes."

"But what if something happens later?" she asked.

"The lens might be found in a can in a month, in five years, or never at all. If it were delivered to a bar, no one would even notice it. The chef would simply throw it away and not bother with it. A drunken customer wouldn't notice it, or if he did, he'd blame the chef. Even if it was sent to a hospital, it might not be noticed. While we wait to see if it's discovered, our situation might change. Don't you think?" The female worker nodded slowly, as though she understood for the first time that the cans, once sealed, might never be reopened.

Four months had passed since the plant manager's disappearance. During that time, an order was returned to the company. The returned cans had been processed around the time the manager disappeared. A customer who bought a can of mackerel from a supermarket found a blob of something red in it. She thought it might be the blood from the mackerel, but she felt uncomfortable and reported it to the authorities. Analysis revealed that it was human blood, and this sparked an investigation. It was concluded that a worker had injured a finger during processing and blood from the wound had got into the can. However, no one had been injured in the factory, and there was no procedure that would have caused such a bloody injury. Even if such an injury were possible, a worker bleeding that much wouldn't have gone unnoticed. Over fourteen hundred cans had been produced that day. Some of them were returned, but most of them were not. Among those returned, some cans contained a great deal of blood, some had very little, some none at all.

The director explored every possible method for shortening the stop work order that the authorities had imposed on the company. He frowned at the mere mention of the human blood incident. He was exhausted. His eyes reddened. The manager of general affair's face reddened whenever he had to deal with the director's anger, which didn't dissipate, even when the stop-work period finally expired.

*

The plant manager had left few possessions. There was little else besides his work clothes, some old underwear, and a few street clothes. One trunk was enough to hold everything. His wife removed the cans from the kitchen cabinet and dresser and gave them all to Park. She somberly refused even the few souvenir cans that had been prepared especially for her.

"My child and I don't eat canned foods. One day we opened a jackmackerel can and found…" She seemed repelled by the memory. "…we found a dead dog. Ever since then, my child has detested cans." She paused. "That reminds me. We received a package a few days after the news that my husband was missing. I opened the cans in the package and found they were actually cans of jackmackerel and mackerel. Despite their labels, I thought they would be cans of kimchi, radish kimchi, and the like. I wondered why he sent them to us, knowing that we wouldn't eat them."

She stared at Park.

He stared back at her.

"Someday, won't we at least find his body?" she asked sadly.

"Why do you ask that? He might just be hiding out some-where for a while, or…"

"You know that's not the kind of person he is."

Park couldn't find the words to reply.

After the plant manager's wife returned to T country, Park moved into her husband's company housing unit. He had only small boxes to move, just a few pieces of underwear and light clothing, for which two bureau drawers were quite sufficient. He placed several cans in the remaining one, and they rattled when he opened and closed the drawer. Among those cans left behind by his predecessor, he found some whose expiration dates had passed, others that were close to their expiration dates, and some that still had a ways to go. He devoted a while to organizing them by type, expiration date, and size.

The director gave Park the vacant plant manager position.

After he became plant manager, Park began coming to work earlier than any of the others. In the factory, with no one around, he turned on the electricity to wake the motionless machinery, which seemed to him like waking a sleeping dog. Then, like a barking dog, the machinery produced a loud, harsh roar, which felt to him like the start of the day.

He also began leaving later than all the others. Turning off the electricity and standing there in the silence at the end of the working day, he felt like a jackmackerel or a mackerel in a can. He carried this feeling with him as he returned to his company housing and drowned himself in wine in order to get to sleep.

Now that he arrived earlier and left later than the others, the workers called him the janitor. He ignored this.

One morning he decided he should have breakfast so that he wouldn't have to start his day so early on an empty stomach. It was a long time until lunch, and besides, he had a sour stomach from his hangover. Hesitantly, he took a can from one of the drawers and opened it. He chewed the jackmackerel bones and meat for a while and felt the seasoning fill his mouth. The salt and fish gradually saturated his taste buds. It tasted better than he initially thought. As he ate more of it, he tasted more flavor. For lunch he ate canned foods and rice with the workers. After he'd been eating with them for some time, one of the workers looked at him putting a piece of jackmackerel into his mouth and said: "*Ungh*! Mr. Manager, you don't eat canned foods, do you?" Park put a morsel of white rice steeped in fish juice into his mouth, and smiled mischievously. Then having eaten the rice and fish, he ate cans of peaches and oranges. The sweet taste lingered in his mouth even after he brushed his teeth. He felt as though he'd been sucking candy all day long. It wasn't all that bad. Returning home from work, he started opening cans and either cooking the contents with kimchi or mincing them into a seasoned sauce to accompany a drink.

When he'd finished all his cans, he opened one of the former plant manager's cans for the first time and was immediately confused. He looked at the contents. He read the label. They didn't match. He opened all the other cans and burst out laughing. They were an utter mess. None of the labels and contents matched. Opening jackmackerel cans, he found not only jackmackerel but also mackerel or sesame leaves. Opening mackerel cans, he found mackerel or sesame leaves or jackmackerel. The same was true for the fruit cans. Some of them seemed to have been prepared to be sent to T country, as there were beans cooked in soy sauce, stir-fried anchovies, or mildewed and sour mashed potatoes that had been marinated and cooked a long time ago. Everything that had been sealed in these cans was meant to have been kept secret until the cans were opened. While eating mackerel from a jackmackerel can, or beans cooked in soy sauce from a mackerel can, or sesame leaves from a sesame leaf can, Park realized it was the first time he'd ever laughed because of something the former plant manager had done.

The cans also contained inedible items. There were dirty socks and disgustingly smelly underwear. There were several detailed statements for transferring money to T country and several English letters his daughter had written him from there as well as several months of paystubs, statements of installment payments he was making for his pension and life insurance, and a key chain with the plant manager's initials tied to another key chain with another person's initials. Park found credit card statements and scrutinized them. They included detailed information from long ago, revealing, for example, that the plant manager had eaten in a restaurant with someone, drank tea, and gone to a cinema. Park paid close attention to specific information of this kind, but he felt uncomfortable about it. Without intending to, he felt he'd become involved in the former manager's private life.

Then, once, when he was about to open a can, he felt suddenly frightened. So far his experience had taught him that he could never guess what he was going to discover in the next can. It occurred to him that one day he might even find bloody, rotten, malodorous bits of unidentifiable bones and flesh. The former plant manager had told him he'd once sealed a dead dog in a can, after all. Park grappled with the thought, and decided he'd take this can to the factory. He'd get a larger can, and being careful not to get blood on his hands, he'd transfer the contents, and press the lid down to seal it. When the air in the can was sucked out with a whooshing sound, the rotting bones and flesh would be sealed in again for a time, still silently keeping their secret. It would be the first time Park had hermetically sealed anything other than jackmackerel or mackerel. He reached for a knife, slowly opened the can, and stared at the contents. He realized that quite probably this was what the former plant manager had done.

In the Hell of Monotony
Kim Hyeong-jung

Desperate Construction

IN PYUN HYE YOUNG's second collection of short stories, *To the Kennels*, I came upon a man who was working on a construction project under cover of darkness. He was erecting a wall. But reading carefully, I knew it was a desperate work of construction because the existence of human civilization seemed to depend on the success or failure of his work. Why did he work on it every night? He wanted to prevent weeds, winged insects, and field mice from invading his house, and also to erect a solid boundary between the wetland and his yard.

> He wanted to build the wall quickly. He wanted to build a solid house free of weeds, winged insects, or field mice. He wanted to wipe out the weeds that obscured the clear boundary between the house and the wetland. He wanted to dig a tumulus in the back of his house and fill the wetland with it. Alternatively he thought about abandoning the house and running away.
> ("Night's Construction," from *Toward the Kennels*, Munhakdongnae, 2007, 111)

At that time rodents appeared frequently in Pyeon Hye Young's stories. (Lemmings, sewer mice, field mice, as well as dogs, cats, birds, and humans are all depicted as rodents in Pyun's work). But let's leave this aside and look cautiously at the shape of the wetland. Pyun's earlier books were dominated by the *Kulong Kulong* sound, emanating from rotting reservoirs, garbage dumps from which black waters flow, damp wetlands, menstrual blood in discarded cloth, and the water and odor from abandoned corpses, etc. These grotesque images provoke disgust but at the same time they strangely entice us. We recoil while still wishing to experience them. They evoke a queer dual sense of attachment and disgust similar to the feeling we have when we look at our own excrement.

> Most of the Water-shield or Hydrilla verticillata were darkly dead already and floating rootless. The surface stayed unmoved by the wind. The mucilaginous, mushy masses filled the wetland. It was like a hard concrete wall in the sense that it kept anyone from approaching. The surface moved occasionally when my wife threw a field mouse, coiling its tail, caught from the house, or when the sewer water poured out of the sewer pipe coming from the village. At such times the wetland momentarily moved, signaling that all was going well. Then the fathomless pothole revealed its dark inside. The open pothole reminded him of his wife's pubes. It was the bottomless and odorous hole of entangled dark and dirty hair. He avoided it as much as he could.
> ("Night's Construction," 96)

Now, having pored over Pyun's stories, I'd say that the displeasing feeling from the wetland (the reservoir, pothole, and corpses of "Ashes and Red") itself emerges from an irreducible mucilaginous substance of some kind. Cha Miryeong, commenting on "Ashes and Red," invokes what Julia Kristeva called "the abject," that is to say an experience of an amorphous substance without boundary or contour, unable to be intellectually defined and delimited as an object. As every modern man seemingly should be, the man in "Ashes and Red" is afraid of such an experience. Facing the overflowing substances presented in the story, the boundaries between the controlling subject and its objects are neutralized, and one feels the fear and discomfort of being enticed by those unstable objects. This man's construction work therefore shouldn't be underestimated as merely a matter of erecting a wall. It is the most basic effort humans have made since the birth of civilization to maintain that civilization. Formless nature, so often called "savage," was once humankind's placenta, upon which they eventually labored to make order, to make distinctions between human habitation and savage habitation, between cosmos and chaos. Thus the man's determined work, while an act of desperation, is the very act upon which human life depends.

This is why Pyun's earlier books treat mice, bushes and thick woods ("Woods in the West") as being scarier than a wolf or an elephant that has escaped from the zoo. The wolves and elephants have separate living spaces to distinguish them from humans. The zoo reminds humans that we are well secured by spatial divisions. This human victory is proudly displayed in "The Birth of a Zoo" and "Parade," for example. Therefore the zoo isn't a place where humans truly preserve and memorialize their lost wildness. This has always been a deception, as is shown in "Masqueraded Utopia." Civilized nature is no longer nature but has become a part of civilization. The zoo animals aren't there to make us feel afraid but to stimulate our nostalgia and stir up our sense of victory.

Weeds and woods, however, are scary. Rodents, as in "Manhole" from *Ashes and Red*, are even scarier because they do not stay outside the boundaries that humans have set for civilization. To our discomfort, they cross all the boundaries, divisions and orders. It is as though they prove the fact that the oppressed will emerge eventually, no matter how humans conquer and control nature. The most fearful things on earth are those things that spread and thrive anywhere, anytime. Weeds and rodents belong to this category of fearful things, those that destroy boundaries.

So now several years have passed since the man's work started, and we may wish that his work will be successful in Pyun's new story collection, *Evening Proposal*. Let us wish that his house, the human space, and the wetland, the rodent' space, will be differentiated and in proper order. Let us hope that the differentiating system won't collapse, and that those strange, terrifying, enticing objects won't return. As we know, the man drowned with his wife in the wetland. His unfinished work made the matter worse, as the wall was removed completely, leaving no trace of a boundary. The deluged wetland flowed more widely, solidly and slowly. If the construction work fails again, humans will fall back into a savage condition.

What Garden City?

Reading carefully, however, I see a man in *Evening Proposal* still hopelessly taking a walk in darkness. His walk could be viewed as a kind of construction work, too, in that he also wants to protect his family and home (a garden city home) from a dog and a wild boar. He attempts to avoid the hell that mingles nature and civilization without distinguishing between them. A solemn and justifiable attempt, but he makes mistakes. He mistakes the garden city for true nature. He overlooks the fact that the garden city is just another term for oppressed nature, the savage that is ready to seek revenge against the civilization that has sought to control it. The man underestimates nature.

> "It would be a change. We'd live somewhere else for a little while. It shouldn't be so bad," she said, looking around the house where they'd lived since getting married. He felt a slight stirring in his heart. He felt that his work and his relationship with his wife had been following a repetitive operation manual. Familiar and comfortable, but it had become boring and uninteresting to the degree that insensitivity wasn't even an issue. He now read similar sentiments in his wife's face as she glanced absentmindedly around the house. They easily agreed to relocate.
> ("Out for a Walk," 95)

The man and his wife in the story have "easily agreed" that they wanted to leave for a garden city to escape the tedium of a "a repetitive operation manual." So he naively crosses the boundary of civilization and is punished. This time it isn't by rodents but by mayflies—creatures commonly thought of as trivial or of no consequence. We speak of the ephemeral life of mayflies, but perhaps they shouldn't be considered so harmless. For Pyun, mayflies, like many other creatures, cause the same deep terror as weeds, woods, and rodents.

> He didn't realize until he was out of breath that he couldn't escape from them no matter how fast he ran because they weren't merely chasing him. They were swarming all over him. They were nesting in him. There was no way that he could escape them or defeat their solid community.
> ("Out for a Walk," 110)

Alone in the woods on a darkening mountain path, the man
is completely surrounded by mayflies, so that he seems to be
living an even more ephemeral life than the insect's. Here, we
see the fiercest mayflies in the history of Korean fiction—not
because they make our skin itchy, or because their attack is fatal,
but because they're swarming all over our land—going inside,
beyond the boundary that forms us. They're in our eyes, noses
and ears. They spread everywhere, invading the boundary and
breaking the contract (albeit a one-sided and partial contract).
They ignore the tens of thousands of years of divided construction that humans have worked on. Moreover, dark clouds,
shrubs, unrecognizable plants, the sounds of the wild boar and
the dead dog's gaze assist them. After the familiar orders have
completely collapsed, overwhelming fear comes over the man.
A world without discernment is a hell to humans.

Thus the thing he finally misses is a well-planned, well-organized, artificial nature, and the sounds of urban civilization. And
what he admits finally is the fact that "he was lost in a completely
unfamiliar world" ("Out for a Walk," 109). It isn't simply out
of the ordinary. It's "completely unfamiliar." What he expects
from a garden city—as modern people often expect—is peaceful
nature with a clear sky and clean air. However, nature is, as usual,
and despite tens of thousands of years of work, in total opposi-
tion (*tout autre*) to humans. In the end, he finds the maze in the
woods. It seems natural for him to get lost in the maze, with
nowhere to turn, since the city has already become a monotonous
hell, and the garden city, with its world of omnipresent mayflies,
weeds, and shrubs, has erased all differentiation. Based on this
story, I'd say that the author finds the construction of differentiation, despite all of humanity's expectation, to br hopeless. The
oppressed ones will inevitably respond by wiping out all order

and all difference. Mayflies and rodents will never go away. The continuous work has become useless, as always.

Circumstantially, however, the end of his life in the woods—when it looks as though he dies in the confusion that nature brought to him—seems not totally devoid of meaning. His ending in the forest maze leaves us with an important clue to understanding Pyun Hye Young's *Evening Proposal* collection. Before his death, the man clarifies the "labyrinth" motive (which has appeared briefly in her former stories, "Picnic" and "Woods in the West," from *To the Kennels*).

> The farther he walked, the denser the pine forest became. He continued on for some time, until the forest turned into something completely different. Sharp tree branches began to strike him. Bushes and trees of every size surrounded him. He wondered if he was going around in circles, returning again and again to the same place. It was like a sense of déjà vu. The deeper the forest became, the more the trails looked the same. Everywhere he saw tall trees that blocked out the sky, he heard the ominous cries of birds, and felt high, hard weeds sticking him through his long pants. The trails were barely connected, then suddenly disconnected, then reconnected by the trodden-down grass.
>
> ("Out for a Walk," 108)

Pyun Hye Young's definition of maze isn't "unfamiliar roads" but "very familiar roads." Those phrases, "going around in circles, returning again and again to the same place," "a sense of déjà vu," and "everywhere he saw the tall trees that covered the sky," indicate that he gets lost because the roads are too familiar to discern one from another. Actually, humans, or even animals, would hardly get lost on "different roads." Road signs, signature

stones or landmarks indicate one direction or the other and differentiate one place from another. As the structuralists say, "In
the beginning there was the structure," which means that in
the beginning there was "difference," which made the world an
object of discernment. Therefore, contrary to common opinion, the maze isn't an unfamiliar situation but the very familiar
monotonous repetition that deranges our sense of geography. So
this man on his walk could be said, like the other, to have been
attacked by the wetland and reservoir. The power of nature, chaos
itself, wipes out all possibility of differentiation and gives him
the last breath of his life. As he breathes his last, he misses "the
air pollution, the identical trees lining the streets at regular intervals, the slices of sky visible between the skyscrapers" ("Out for
a Walk," 110). This paradoxically speaks of how much he wants
differentiation and order as he faces the terror of monotony. He
should have stayed in the city where well-organized orderliness
reigns rather than hastily desiring the garden city.

Predictably, almost all the stories in *Evening Proposal* except
"Out for a Walk" are about people who decide to live in the
city as it is. There, nature becomes the background scenery or is
removed as though it never existed. There isn't any walk, garden
city, picnic, or zoo. The problem, however, is that the labyrinth
motif appears in almost all Pyun's stories. Now then the maze
is no longer nature's revenge against civilization or a response
from the oppressed. The maze is made by civilization itself.
Civilization itself becomes the hell of monotony.

Consequently the grotesque objects from Pyun's earlier novels,
for instance, the corpses, rubbish, and foul odor, now disappear.
The wetland seems to become a dry desert maze. Nonetheless
Pyun's stories are still uncomfortable and terrifying, and Shin
Hyeong-cheol justifiably says that Pyun changes direction "from
the grotesque to the uncanny." Now it is no longer grotesque

nature's recurrence that is the object of terror, but daily living on the whole that estranges and drops us into the uncanny maze. *Evening Proposal* renews the warning that the orderliness and systematization that civilization created in order to confront nature's chaos is in fact "the hell of monotony" that humans abhor. The civilization constructed to confront the savage will, in the end, itself become savage. Enlightened reason's control over nature will finally return to the savage condition. This prophecy by Ado Reno is being renewed in this Pyun Hye Young's story collection.

In the Copy Room

Looking into *Evening Proposal*, I see the poorest of all men is the man in "Monotonous Lunch," who eats the same lunch at the same place each day. His life is a compressed version of the lives of all the rest of the protagonists in the stories (and actually of the lives of most of the people who are reading this commentary).

> Perhaps it was eating the same meal every day that also deceived him into thinking that today was the same as yesterday, and that tomorrow night would be no different than tonight. Perhaps it prevented him from realizing that days and nights were passing differently for other people, while he was shut away in his basement copy room. His daily life was exactly like the Set A menu that, with a few small changes, was basically, perpetually the same. It consisted of always rising at the same time, dressing in the same blue or black outfits, taking the same commuter rail every morning and evening, and working the same regular business hours in his copy room.
> ("Monotonous Lunch," 50)

Of course Pyun Hye Young's hard-boiled phrases don't allow comparisons or rhetorical expressions, so it can't really be conveyed, through this summary alone, with what detail and dryness the author displays this man's boring daily life. Adding a few more words, we say that this man reads bound books, regardless of content, and the following is what he does all day:

He took their material, set the machine to copy and pressed the green button to start copying. And:

the bright light flashed, he averted his eyes to look at the empty wall, the bookshelf, or the alley.

Then, when his copying is done:

He handed over the copied material, usually received paper money in payment, fumbled in the can for change, and sat back down in his chair. He repeated this sequence dozens of times a day.
("Monotonous Lunch," 55).

Even when he witnesses the suicide in the subway, he refuses the policeman's request to testify so that he can get to the copy room on time and maintain his inertia by repeating this meaningless routine. He is totally captured by the daily monotony; it becomes more important than another person's death. Without exception, at lunchtime, even if he isn't hungry, he goes to the cafeteria to eat the same Set A lunch. This is how Pyun Hye Young describes his daily life.

The Set A Lunch at noon had divided his day into two parts, morning and afternoon. But it wasn't only morning and afternoon that were divided in this way. Yesterday and today were divided by midnight. Last week and this week were divided by the weekend. Last year and this year were divided by the end of the year. The future would always be divided from the past, the present divided from the past, and the future from the present. It would always be this way. Thinking this he sighed, but he also felt relieved. He stopped sighing. ("Monotonous Lunch," 64)

And like the monotonous lunch that divides his morning and afternoon, his daily life piles up like sheets of paper for a bookbinding. The story begins with his eating lunch and ends with his eating lunch. "Rabbit's Tomb," "Canning Factory," and "Would You Like to Take a Tour Bus?" also take this structure, a form very appropriate for the subject of repetition. Of course, before the end of the story, his foreseeable future is included as follows.

He suddenly became aware of the cold air of the basement copy room and knew he'd spend his entire future there. He would from time to time get a paper cut, and that was the only kind of scar he'd ever have. In the warmth of the copy machine's radiant light, he'd find comfort in this scar, and he'd always, quite precisely, make change with nickels and pennies. ("Monotonous Lunch," 60)

By the way, is this a prediction or a condemnation? In the same space, keeping the same schedule, eating the same meal, wearing the same clothes, reading the same bound books, coming to work and going home via the same transportation, without any difference or fluctuation, so that the past, the present, and the future are exactly the same, this life of continuous sameness—that is the "copy of life." And this "hell of monotony" is even more terrifying than the terror caused by the reservoir, the wetland, field mice, corpses, rubbish, bad odors, and mayflies.

Looking more carefully, I see the lifestyle of the director, the plant manager, Park, and the other workers as all being the same. They eat three meals a day, eat canned food, turn on the machinery at the same hour, put the same stuff into cans, and suffer the same anxiety and hardships of living. One of them may die and disappear from the system, or make some big or small mistake. Nevertheless, the repetition continues. When the plant manager disappears, Park becomes plant manager. When Park disappears, someone else (one of those who made and ate the same canned food) will become plant manager. Then he will eat the same canned food, turn on the machinery at the same hour, and make the same canned food. Time and space can't escape from this controlling sameness.

Again looking carefully I see the lives of the protagonists in "Rabbit's Tomb" and "Jungle Gym" are no different from the life of the rabbit which was taken care of during the workers' dispatched periods and then abandoned. Like the man, all are dispatched workers, who don't know exactly what they are doing, without whom the company runs just as well, and whose disappearance leaves no trace. And even if one escapes the hell of monotony, there is nowhere else but home to go. One may take a journey by chance, but this only becomes a way to find a maze in which one wanders meaninglessly. Even if one stays at home like everyone else, one is assured of the same repetition.

Again looking in carefully, I see in the story "Evening Proposal" that even love won't change the future from becoming the same as the present. The present, the future, life, and death are all homogeneous, so we live and will die exactly as we are. If by chance one could have escaped from this daily repetition, as Jin does, the protagonist in "Room with a Beige Sofa" who was drowned in the regional highway's pothole, never to return, the hell of monotonous living comes to seem like a comfort.

In short, Pyun's characters, trapped in the repetitions of space and time, find their proper environment in the maze and the reservoir. Maze and reservoir, even if they are or appear to be divided into civilization and nature, the familiar and the confrontational, share the hell of monotony. The savage is civilization. Civilization is the savage. Pyun Hye Young's third story collection sends us this warning.

Welcome To Hardboiled Hell!

Again, coming back to "Night's Construction," we find the man's work is a complete failure by the time we reach *Evening Proposal*. It was already a failed work, but now the hell of monotony that he was so afraid of and that he tried so desperately to prevent until his death, becomes not only the territory of oppressed nature symbolized by the reservoir, but also expands its territory into the city civilization, the order and differentiation one trusted to exist. Nature, civilization, and the garden city all become hell. There is no escape because in Pyun Hye Young's stories the future is the same as the present.

For that reason, it doesn't seem easy for anyone to predict what Pyun's next world will be like. Having seen her tough spirit, we can't expect that she will show us how to escape from this hell. Perhaps a more horrible hell will better fit her style, and this would align well with the general prospects of Korean literature. It also suits our present life, in which infectious diseases and all kinds of disasters predominate. It won't be easy or pleasant to imagine the more horrible hell Pyun is going to show us.

When *Aoi Garden* (2005) was first published, the critic Lee Gwang-ho greeted the nightmarish stories with, "Welcome to Hard Gore Wonderland!" Pyun's novels no longer seem to depend on hard gore imagination. I feel, however, that *Evening Proposal* is even more eerie and scary. What is more scary than the savage's revenge or oppressed nature's recuperation is the fact that our civilization, warm and cozy, is itself already a savage nature, and a hell of monotony, permitting no differentiation. It is time to change Gwang-ho's welcome, although none of us will like this, but to all of us who read Pyun Hye Young's third story collection:

"Welcome to Hardboiled Hell!"

Author's Words

IT BEGAN LIKE this. S, being in a hurry, took a taxi. The driver was changing radio stations, and on one of the programs S heard a story told by a member of the audience. Meanwhile I was at a library, idly leafing through an art book, and I paused to look at a painting on one of its pages. We were always planning to leave for somewhere, so we finally took off for Tongyeong. We got lost and found an old factory on a road we happened to go down. Y started talking. In a Shinagawa Residence elevator, I met a grim-faced neighbor and felt nervous all the way up to the sixth floor. Walking aimlessly around a tourist district, I passed by the same road again and again. Each time I saw a jungle gym unusually placed in the middle of the road. After a long search in an unfamiliar area, an older colleague, having only an address, finally found it and was met by a huge dog. A younger colleague of S's bought a book that listed movies, and was watching the movies in it one by one. After reading about a singer who died a long time ago, I searched for her songs, listened to them, and understood only one phrase.

This book contains all of these incidents. I still enjoy seeing accidental encounters like these grow into stories whether they turn out to actually have happened or not.

Writing fiction always requires a great deal of labor, and I realize how this has changed me somewhat. How it has made me feel less shame and despair. Little by little, I've come to better understand the silent training that writing fiction provides.

It is my longtime habit to think about the process of labor when I look at an item. Whenever I look at this book, it will always remind me of the labor provided by the Munhak-gwa-Jiseong-Sa members. I am grateful to them. I am also grateful to those anonymous people who are dispatched to strange places and then return to the places they left behind.

Pyun Hye Young
March 2011

These stories were first published in the following magazines:

Modern Literature, March 2009: "Rabbit's Tomb"
Author's World, Winter 2009: "Evening Proposal"
Korean Literature, Winter 2008: "Monotonous Lunch"
Literature of the World, Autumn 2008: "Would You Like to Take a Tour Bus?"
Literature and Society, Spring 2008: "Out for a Walk"
Literature Notebook, Spring 2009: "Jungle Gym"
One Day Seoul Became a Novel, Kang 2009: "A Room with Beige Couch"
Literature Village, Summer 2009: "Canning Factory"